The Duke Beneath Her Mistletoe

by

Nicki Pascarella

Christmas in the Castle Series

Cover Art by *The Wild Rose Press, Inc.*

The Wild Rose Press, Inc.
PO Box 708
Adams Basin, NY 14410-0708
Visit us at www.thewildrosepress.com

Publishing History
First Edition, 2023
Trade Paperback ISBN 978-1-5092-5313-5
Digital ISBN 978-1-5092-5315-9

Christmas in the Castle Series
Published in the United States of America

They stood in the center of the makeshift *piste*, Georgie facing William as the man fluttered his thick lashes. If it were not for the blunted weapon, she would have sliced the damnable black fans off. She brought the blade to her face, then forward and down.

William languidly repeated the salute.

The man deserved to be run through, not treated like an honorable opponent. The Duke of Astleyshire was about to learn the most important lesson of his life—never underestimate the fighting skill of a woman.

Georgie channeled one of her heroines, the agile Signora Ermenegilda Cheli. Knees bent, right foot forward, weapon steady, her back arm raised, she prepared.

"En garde!"

Her sword extended as she lunged. Still smirking and straight-legged, William parried as if he were swatting a fly. Georgie growled. Back foot first, she slid until she was a safe distance away, then rethought her strategy. Resting the point of his blade against the ballroom floor, William crossed one foot over the other and again fluttered his lashes.

What the bloody hell?

"Don't be a fool, Astleyshire. She will run you through like a Turkish kebab," Stephen called.

Praise for Nicki Pascarella

This novella was fun, fast-paced, and sexy as hell... Thanks for showing me all the perks of reading a novella, Nicki...
—*Steamy Cairo Nights* reviewer, Smutty Book Reviews

"Pascarella has a dynamite series in the Miranda Albright, Ph.D books. These books are for the reader who wants it all, mystery mixed with humor, topped with steamy romance. Her small town is full of quirky characters the reader will never forget."
—Marilyn Barr, author

Dedication

To Kyann Waters
Thank you for believing in me and being such an
amazing critique partner.

Chapter One

December 14th, 1816

Jackson Valiant pressed the point of his sword into Baron Goldcount's neck. "You will not touch Maria Seraphina again. For if you do, I will slice you into a hundred pieces and invite the wild wolves who live in the surrounding forest to a feast."

This was no idle threat because the heroic Jackson did indeed control the hungry pack.

From Tattle's Tales

The Duke of Astleyshire plastered on his sultry smile and swaggered into his third ball of the holiday season. Thirty seconds after his entrance, an attractive woman halted him with the tip of her fan. The widowed countess skimmed a gloved finger over his forearm as she leaned close to whisper, "Your Grace, I do hope that we are able to take a turn in the garden later this evening."

Since Lady Hemmingsworth was a skilled lover, and her raspy voice was akin to having his balls caressed, William Harrington winked. "Very soon, Susana."

Taking his leave, he navigated a thousand crystal snowflakes, dozens of girls smiling behind fluttering ivory fans, and a sea of husband-seeking mothers to peacock to the Prince Regent.

"Good evening, Your Royal Highness." William swept into his most elegant bow.

"William." The prince's eyes were slits atop swollen cheeks, but his voice was genuine and affable. "I am glad you are here. I need a trustworthy ear."

"I as well." Despite his social exhaustion, and desire to leave London and return to his family seat, William oozed charm. "How is my dear aunt?"

"Between you and I, the queen is quite bored." The prince shoved an entire iced pastry into his mouth and swallowed with ease. "Let us find a quiet place to talk. I have had enough of this." He waved wiggling fingers toward the orchestra plucking from the stage centered on a faux lake.

William allowed his older cousin to lean on him as the two men, followed by a half dozen of the prince's entourage, navigated the bowing and curtseying *ton*.

As the prince engaged in small talk, William reminisced about a younger, less corpulent man who had played energetic games of pall mall with him when he was a child. Too much of everything, from food, to ale, to women had taken their toll.

The prince hesitated in front of a door and wheezed. "Lord Lionel will not mind if we use his study." Using his sleeve, he wiped beads of sweat from his brow.

They entered the room and William helped his cousin to sit, then lit two candelabra.

His face flushed, the prince panted. "I am sorry for the loss of your father. He was a good man, a loving uncle, and a friend to the Crown."

William swallowed. Two months had passed, and

he still struggled to talk about his father's death. He knew better than to ask after the king's health. It was a sensitive subject to his family and a few years prior, he had bloodied the Marquess of Birmington's oldest son's nose for calling his uncle Ol' Mad an' Batty.

"The late Duke of Astleyshire was instrumental in passing the Frame-Breaking Act. I hope we can count on you to continue in his footsteps," the prince said.

"Of course."

William dreaded politics. But his carefree days of gambling, drinking, womanizing, and sport had come to an end the second his father passed, and he inherited a dukedom. Well, almost come to an end. It was the holiday season, and no man was perfect.

"I knew I could count on you." The prince cupped a hand to his ear, then crooked a finger, beckoning William to lean close. "Have you heard of this Winkentattle who is writing chapbooks for the working class?"

"I have," William said. Although he ignored the rumblings since silly stories printed on small scraps of paper were of no interest to him.

"Baron Handershane was a dear friend of your father's," the prince said.

The newly appointed baron made William's skin crawl, and he avoided the man as if he carried the pox.

"He believes these chapbooks could cause a repeat of the attack on Cartwright's Mill near Cleckheaton."

If William's memory was correct, a few years earlier, working-class men had been hanged for breaking equipment in protest of their poor working conditions.

"You would think that would have been an end to

the troubles, but there is to be another Luddite hanging at Derby Gaol in a couple of weeks," the prince said.

William schooled his cringe. He knew little about this group of people fighting against progress and causing upheaval. But hangings were never a good thing.

"Rumor has it that this Winkentattle is operating out of Trent Village and targeting Handershane's mill. Since you are not far from there, and I trust you implicitly, I hope you might look into this matter. I have a dear friend who does love the lace made at Handershane's factory, and one must keep the fairer sex happy." The prince winked and hacked.

Bloody hell. Spying for the Crown? William had simply wanted to say hello to his cousin then plant himself deep inside a warm woman.

"Yes. One must keep the ladies happy," William agreed with a forced smile. "However, I am unsure how I can help with this matter. Hockley Castle is a half-hour ride from Trent Village on a clear summer day."

"But you and Alistair Eaton are old friends. Roommates at Bedford and Cambridge if I remember correctly."

"Yes," William said.

"Then visit him at his family seat and see what you can learn about this Winkentattle." The prince chuckled. "But keep away from that hellcat sister of his. The queen fears the lady is a blemish on genteel society. Handershane claims it took all three of her brothers to keep her from scratching his eyes out the last time he visited Trent Castle."

An on-the-shelf sister who scratched out men's eyes? A repugnant baron? One of his cousin's greedy mistresses? Could the night get any worse?

William assisted the prince when he struggled to stand.

"I trust that you will make your father proud." The prince clapped him on the shoulder. "And now that I have made my appearance, I will take my leave. I look forward to hearing from you. After Twelfth Night, I plan to return to Brighton and hope to relay excellent news to my friend, letting her know that her lace shall be in good supply this season." The prince gazed over William's head. Perhaps he was revisiting precious memories. "Dictating the season's fashion is only one of her many charms."

Once the door closed, William collapsed onto his chair and moaned.

The bottle of port on the desk called to him. He poured himself a glass and chugged. His father's words on his deathbed echoed as the liquid burned his esophagus.

"Son, your duties are now to your country and your dukedom. Make me proud."

He poured and swallowed a second glass. Then a third.

The door opened and Lord Lionel stepped into the room. "Astleyshire?"

William stood, and his world completed one full spin, tilted, then righted itself. Mayhap he had drunk too much.

"Forgive me," William said. "His Royal Highness needed a quiet place to rest. He just left. I hope that it is of no consequence that I helped myself to a drink."

Lord Lionel's gaze slid to the almost empty decanter.

"A few drinks," William confessed.

"I dare say. You look as though you have had a rough evening."

William faked a chuckle. "I am fine."

"Sit, my good man. A few of us plan to enjoy the remainder of the evening in a game of cards. Lady Lionel is preoccupied and will not notice my absence."

The door flew open, and four men barged into the room.

"Sorry to hear about your father, Astleyshire," Lord Beers said.

No matter how many times he heard the sentiment, it left William at a loss for words.

Despite his protests, William found himself seated at a table, a fresh drink in front of him, and cards in his hands.

Unfortunately, his friend's younger brother sat beside him. He'd disliked Evan Eaton the first time Alistair introduced them. The boy had been an obnoxious, energetic little thing, running amok in their dormitory while asking too many questions. Now he was a pompous arse who flirted with William's conquests.

"Evan," Lord Lionel said, "I am sorry that Lord Trent was not able to join us. Please send him my regards."

"The Dowager Countess Trent arrived at Trent Castle this evening and my brother and sister stayed to greet her. The Lady Eatons cannot be left together. They require a chaperone." Evan Eaton rolled his eyes. "Make that a lion tamer. *Whipsh!*" he said, as his hand snapped forward.

William recoiled at the crack of the pretend whip.

Evan pointed at William and chuckled. "A bit jumpy, Your Grace? Mayhap you need to slow down on the libations."

Evan Eaton could bugger off. William tilted his head back and emptied his glass.

The toothless first son of the Marquess of Birmington, Thomas Merrick, chortled. "Evan, how is that sister of yours?"

Evan's elbow hit the table and a card fluttered, landing beside William's boot. The youngest Eaton sibling smirked. "She is busy planning your demise, Thomas."

The other men were so busy guffawing that they did not notice Evan's turn of the wrist when he bent forward.

"What the bloody hell did you just retrieve from the floor?" William asked Evan.

"My bleeding card, Duke. You have had enough to drink," Evan shot back.

William showered Evan with all of the contempt he could muster. How in the hell could he visit Alistair if the cheater and the hellcat came with Trent Castle?

Fifteen minutes and another drink later, William had enough. Evan Eaton was a no-good cheat.

"Pay up, Eaton," William demanded, holding out his palm and shoving it in the rogue's face.

Evan slapped a hand on the table. "That is the second time tonight you have cheated and blamed me." Evan glared at every man in the room. "I know he is a bloody duke, but will anyone stand up to him?"

Evan Eaton tossed coins onto the table. Thereupon he huffed and slammed the door behind him.

"And I have to spend the holidays with the

bastard." William blinked. Had he said that out loud?

Thomas laughed. "Mayhap the dashing duke should try his hand at the spinster while he is visiting Trent Castle."

A chorus of "Hear, hear!" and pounding fists erupted.

William was not in the mood, and the next cockchafer who called him *the dashing duke* might end up with a fist in his mouth. He grabbed a decanter and poured. "Not interested."

"I hear she does not like men. Have you ever heard anything so shocking? A chit who does not like men. Just ask Lord Kingsley."

It did not matter who said it. At that moment, the chuckling thingamabobs were all rotten bastards.

William's tongue had developed a mind of its own and stuck to his palate, making conversation almost impossible. "S-she would damn well like *me*."

He winced. What would make him say such a foolish thing? Pride? Arrogance? Bloody alcohol? He pushed his glass to the center of the table.

"Ah," said Thomas. "Care to wager? Fifty pounds says Lady Georgiana Eaton stabs the Duke of Astleyshire in the heart."

"I'll take that wager and double it. I say she beds-s me within one week," William slurred. "But now, I have to meet someone els-se."

He may have lost his balance once or twice as he excused himself and swayed back to the ballroom.

A blurry Susana Hemmingworth stood against the far wall, giggling at a six-eyed Evan Eaton.

"Hell and damnation." William sloshed to the pair.

"Your Grace." Susana curtsied and smiled.

Eaton, the rake, did not even bother to address him.

William leaned close to the countess's ear and whispered, "Meet me in my carriage in ten minutes-s."

Then he shot Evan a smug smirk. Or it might have been an ungentlemanly vibrating tongue. It was hard to tell much of anything anymore. William pulled his shoulders back and attempted to swagger out of the gathering.

Unfortunately, it took two footmen and an alluring widow to carry him to his carriage.

Chapter Two

Christmas Eve, December 24th, 1816

Wolves snarled as the moonlight reflected off their yellow eyes. Baron Goldcount cowered behind the tree. A lot of good that would do him.
From Tattle's Tales

Georgiana Eaton strategically positioned herself in front of her mattress. Her efforts were pointless since the scowling dowager countess stepped around her and pointed at the lump under the counterpane.

"Georgiana!"

Georgie's shoulders caved as she sighed in resignation. Although relinquishing her copy of *Female Difficulties* was heartbreaking, she had to protect her own writing at all costs. She rooted under the blanket, then placed her beloved Fanny Burney into the countess's hand.

Clucking her tongue, Louisa Eaton pointed at the outline of folded paper still under the fabric. The woman was more stubborn than, well, her. And Georgie had once been told she was as malleable as a brick wall.

Georgie hesitated before reaching between the blankets again. When she did not hand the chapbook over immediately, it was torn from her grasp. She held her breath for an eternity as the frowning woman lifted a lorgnette to her eye and scrutinized the story.

Finally, her grandmother shuddered. "I have heard that Mrs. Burney fills young girls with absurd ideas. And this man is a troublemaker." She waved the newest draft of *Tattle's Tales* about. "Rubbish. Even the paper is chintzy. And to suggest that the working class read and dictate conditions. Why, 'tis preposterous."

Georgie knew the history of her village as well as she knew her own name. In 1811 when workers broke machinery, soldiers had to be called in to stop the riots. This time, she would make sure the demonstrators made their point before soldiers intervened.

"I am of the opinion that everyone should read," Georgie declared. "And as for the paper, many of the villagers can barely afford to eat."

Her grandmother blanched. "It was disastrous. I had to appear at court in a gown I had previously worn because the *modiste* could not obtain the lace for my new one. Sylvia Beaumont has reminded me of it every season since."

"Horrors," said Georgie, sarcasm oozing.

She should grab the old woman by the shoulders and shake sense into her. On a positive note, at least it hadn't occurred to her grandmother that her flesh and blood had penned the "rubbish."

Georgie pulled her shoulders back. "Father allowed me to read in the library with my brothers. No books were off limits." He had also allowed her to write tales of terrifying monsters and bloody battles that would cause the older woman's heart to cease beating.

"It has been too long since a woman has influenced you. My dear son did try his best," the countess said.

Georgie missed her father so much that his

memories knocked the wind from her. Unfortunately, she barely remembered her mother since she had died when Georgie was four.

The dowager countess shook her head, but only slightly. As she often reminded Georgie, "a lady never moves quickly." Unless it was to dramatically fan herself or fall to the ground in a heap of silk and satin. If the latter, she could plummet to the ground like a boulder rolling downhill.

"'Tis a good thing that I am here. I shall school you in the intricacies of behaving like a lady. I will keep you so busy you will no longer concern yourself with radical notions." Whenever her grandmother played God, she lifted her chin until it seemed as if it might reach the ten-foot-high vaulted ceiling. "And, I plan to stay until you receive a worthy proposal."

It would take a massive dose of Christmas spirit to save the holiday.

"Oh, bollocks."

"Georgiana!"

Since the speed of the countess's fanning fingers rivaled hummingbird wings, her prostate body might soon splat on the chamber floor. Unfortunately, if the countess went down, two strong individuals would be required to lift her sturdy frame.

Thank goodness, the door opened, and Millie, with her impeccable timing and crisp blue livery, tip-toed across the carpet and bobbed a curtsey.

"Millie," said the countess in her authoritative voice. "Prepare the pink and silver dress for dinner this evening."

Georgie's nails dug into her fisted palms. "I asked Millie to prepare the royal blue."

Her grandmother held up a long finger. "We are to have an important guest, so you will wear the pink."

The countess—two. Georgie—zero.

Georgie plopped her rump on the mattress. She would wear the pink, but she would *not* spend another season in London being paraded around with a gaggle of ninnies. She would *not* marry some arrogant man and sire his heir. And she *would* read and write. She would hide her habits when in her grandmother's presence. But she was engaging in them, by God!

Her grandmother exhaled, sat on the bed, and placed the confiscated items outside Georgie's grasp. Her tone and expression softened. "The Duke of Astleyshire will dine with us tonight."

Georgie leaped from the bed. "But Christmas Eve is for family. We have the Yule log, dinner, decorating, and the party."

"The duke met with Alistair earlier today, and he will be staying for a sennight." Her grandmother stood slowly, as if lead filled her veins. "'Tis a good thing he arrived when he did, for the weather has taken a turn for the worse."

Georgie rushed to the window. Fluffy flakes fell from the sky, landing on about six inches of fresh snow.

"If he leaves now, he could make it home before the roads become impassable."

She would clear the path herself if she had to. The old wrought iron shovel in the barn should do the trick.

The countess's eyebrows almost reached her gray hairline. "What kind of lady would abandon a duke to the snow?"

Georgie raised her hand.

The older woman *tsk*ed. "With the poor crops and

the unrest at the factories, your family requires His Royal Highness's favor, and His Grace is said to have his ear." She *tsk*ed again. "Do not embarrass your brothers or yourself. I will leave you to your preparations."

How utterly gluttonous! Despite the summer without rain, Georgie's family ate until their bellies were full. They had so much land and money that her brothers and grandmother spent frivolously with little regard for anything. And there were the lavish parties and balls they attended, especially while at their London home!

Halfway to the door, the countess halted her gliding steps. "Millie, please tie Lady Georgiana's hair in the silver ribbon. Make sure to show off her neck and shoulders. She has such lovely shoulders. Just like mine when I was young. I was once quite a beauty." Her grandmother's green eyes looked into the past, and she sighed.

"Yes, my lady." Millie curtsied.

The countess halted before the hearth and tossed Georgie's powerful prose into the roaring fire. The edges turned black, crinkled, then disintegrated.

"I will return this book to the library." With her nose in the air, the countess carried away Fanny.

Once the door closed, Millie reached into her pocket and removed folded papers. "Christopher wants to know what you think of the cover."

Jackson Valiant stood tall, aiming the point of a sword at a corpulent man on his knees. Maria Seraphina's long, brown hair blew about her as if she stood in a windstorm and the hilt of her sword glimmered from above a leather belt cinched around her tiny waist.

Georgie groaned. "I love it, but do they have to make Maria so voluptuous? Speaking of which, I look like a cherry confectionary in the pink. And it makes me—" She waved her hand in front of her bosom, indicating her own overflowing cleavage.

"My lady, this edition is colorful, and Maria looks beautiful." Millie put a hand to her heart and sighed. "And I think pink looks lovely with your red hair. Let us add your pearls."

"The countess is not in the room, so you can stop calling me *my lady*. And do not lie to me. I am dreadful in pink."

Millie opened both doors of the wardrobe to move aside decadent gowns so that she could caress the pink.

Another unfortunate child had probably been sacrificed to the flesh-eating machinery in order to provide the glittery lace adorning the bodice and hem of the absurd frock.

"The countess is not evil. She just wants you to behave like a fine lady so that you make a good match," said Millie.

"*Bluck.*" Georgie's tongue popped out and she rolled her eyes. "I hope she does not think the duke has designs on me. Once he is done sleeping with all of the married women in the *ton*, he will marry a simpering fool like Arabella Beaumont."

Millie's face contorted into one of her disapproving grimaces. "You can't run around in breeches, wrestling with your brothers forever."

"Not with her here filling Alistair's head with nonsense."

Georgie stopped waving her arms to lift them

overhead. Millie helped her out of her mourning dress. Then, bracing her elbows against a bedpost as thick as an oak tree, Georgie prepared for the torture of being imprisoned in her stays.

"The earl asked to see you in his study before dinner," Millie said as she tugged on the laces.

"I wonder what it could be about?"

Millie tugged again.

Georgie spun to face her maid and trusted friend. Yes, her friend. Society be damned.

"Do you think he got me the present I requested? I gave so many hints."

"Jimmy said the earl took him to look at a litter a few days ago." Millie pressed on Georgie's shoulder, turning her back around so that she could tie the final bow. "Mrs. Teague told Cook that the duke looks exceptionally handsome today."

Georgie stepped into her petticoat and wriggled as Millie tied it in place. Pompous William Harrington the Second would not ruin her Christmas eve or sidetrack her from her mission. She and Cook's grandson, twelve-year-old Jimmy, had puppies on the brain.

"Alistair probably has the puppy in his study. What color do you think it is? White? Black? Brown? Short hair or long hair?"

"I could not even guess," said Millie as she deposited satin and lace over Georgie's head and guided it into place.

Georgie plopped down at her dressing table, cringing every time Millie stabbed her with hairpins. Eventually, she relaxed her neck and shoulders and placed a hand on her throat.

"Jackson lifted his sword high and—" She

swallowed and spoke from deep in her diaphragm. "—lifted his sword high and swung." Lowering her pitch even more, her fingers absorbed the reverberation "Swung. Blood trickled."

Millie stopped tugging hair to clap. "Lady Georgiana, you sound like a man and I think this tale is the best yet."

"I need another copy since mine is ash."

Millie bent so that her gaze met Georgie's in the mirror and her cheeks bloomed pink. "In the next story could Jackson kiss Maria?"

Georgie grunted. She had never kissed a man, so she was not certain what all it entailed. Besides, she preferred to think about an adorable bundle of fluff.

"What should I name him? Her?" She turned, knocking her cheek against her maid's hand, sending the silver ribbon fluttering to the ground. "Millie, I just thought of something. If my present is a girl, maybe we will have puppies by next Christmas."

****

Wearing dainty slippers tipped with pink bows, her arms swinging wildly, the normally coordinated Georgie careened down the hall. Light from the sconces reflected off the gilded portraits of her ancestors, giving the castle a warm feel despite the frigid temperatures.

When she reached the stairwell, she exhaled. She gracefully descended three steps. Hopefully, her grandmother was not about because, by the fourth, she hopped like an excited kangaroo.

Plowing into her brother's study, she called out, "Alistair!"

The earl sat behind the ancestral mahogany desk. The firelight cast shadows over his frowning face.

Evan, Georgie's younger brother, reclined in a leather wing-back, a glass of whiskey in one hand and a lit Cheroot in the other. Stunningly handsome, with thick, brown hair and bright, green eyes, his regal posture made him look older than his twenty years.

Although also handsome, Alistair's green eyes did not have the same devilish twinkle. And since his jaw had been clenched since their father's death the previous fall, frown lines had set up permanent residence on his brow.

"Please sit, Georgiana," he said with the stiff formality that seemed to have increased tenfold since inheriting the earldom.

Georgie searched the room for her present. Ceiling-high shelves filled with books. Four reclining chairs with carved arms and fine damask cushions. Rich green draperies hanging to the floor. No puppy.

Alistair cleared his throat. "Georgiana."

Before looking at her older brother, she met Evan's serious gaze and her heart tripped over itself. "Is Stephen well?"

"Stephen? Why would you ask that?" Alistair asked.

"Because Evan looks miserable," she said.

The normally fun-loving Evan snorted. "I am fine. And we have had no news from Stephen. Good, bad, or otherwise. I suppose his regiment is still in France."

The only thing Georgie wanted more than a puppy was for her twin to come home safely. She climbed into the largest chair and swung her legs over the arm. Her feet dangled in the air as she made herself comfortable.

"The three of us need to talk quickly. Grandmother will be joining us any minute," said Alistair.

The back of her neck prickled at the warning. "Proceed."

"Georgiana, your season was a disaster," Alistair said.

So that was the cause of her brothers' long faces. Georgie chortled as her feet fluttered.

"Her last three seasons were disasters." Evan winked at her and chuckled.

Alistair scowled. "Do not encourage her, Evan."

"I had nothing to do with Miss Beaumont's punch-covered gown or Kingsley's injured toe," Evan said.

Georgie had only meant for the red drink to destroy her own gown so she could leave the ball early, but accidentally ruining Arabella Beaumont's in the process was a bonus. And since Lord Kingsley would not stop staring at her *décolletage*, she had used the tip of his walking stick to relocate his gaze.

Alistair groaned, then stood and walked to the window. "The Duke of Astleyshire arrived earlier this afternoon. I asked Mrs. Teague to prepare a room, and I have extended an invitation for him to stay for a week."

"Bollocks," Georgie grumbled, even though she was already privy to the information.

Evan huffed. "Bloody hell. I thought dinner tonight was bad enough."

Alistair turned to glare at his siblings.

"He thinks he is the most handsome man in all of England. In all of the world. I would like to punch him in his nose," Georgie said.

"I would like to knock his high and mighty lordship on his arse. He bilked me last I played cards with him," said Evan. "He was foxed and wore that damn grin the entire time. And then he fucked—"

Alistair cleared his throat.

She was not one for gossip, but Georgie detested the arrogant man. "Whose skirt was he under?" she whispered in case her grandmother was near.

"Enough, both of you. And Georgiana, stop saying unladylike things."

"Oh, bother. Evan can say whatever he likes—"

"No. Evan will refrain from ungentlemanly conversations."

Silence settled over the room.

Eventually, Alistair focused his gaze out the window again. He stood stick-straight, his hands clasped behind his back. "Understand that the countess will stay until Georgiana has a suitable proposal."

Evan took advantage of their older brother's turned back to mouth, "Lady Hemmingsworth."

"But Lady Hemmingsworth is widowed and at least four-and-forty?" Georgie said.

"Georgiana!" Alistair rubbed his temples.

It had to take a lot of effort to constantly reprimand her. *Georgiana, do not do this. Georgiana, do not do that. Georgiana, behave like a lady.* She sighed and tapped Evan on the forearm. He handed over the cigar.

She was attempting not to choke on her puff when Alistair faced them.

He stomped to her, grabbed the Cheroot, and shoved it into his mouth.

"Bloody hell. That is mine. Get your own," Evan grumbled.

"I am trying to talk to you two about something serious," Alistair said.

"Is it my Christmas puppy?" Georgie asked.

"Puppy?" Confusion mingled with Alistair's

intense glare. "No." He shook his head. "I have suggested that Harrington spend time with you, Georgiana. With a chaperone of course. Mayhap there will be a spark, and he will propose."

Georgie's feet hit the ground, and she sat up straight. "What?"

"Georgiana, I have given my blessing for the two of you to court."

"No," she cried, leaping from the chair to rush to him. Looking up into his eyes, she pleaded, "Alistair, please, do not do this to me!"

He placed a hand on her shoulder, and his sad eyes met her gaze. "William has matured. Both of us have left the days of women and drink behind us."

Evan snorted.

"Well, he is less arrogant since his father's death. In fact, he insists we keep our dinner this evening informal and act as if he is not a duke. And, if he does propose, mayhap the countess will return to High Pavement."

For the first time in her life, Georgie thought she might require her grandmother's smelling salts.

Chapter Three

Christmas Eve, December 24th, 1816

Twelve slobbering wolves surrounded Goldcount.
"Bollocks!" How was he to get to his gold and
sausages?
From Tattle's Tales

Despite the heavy tapestries and the plush rugs, the damn parlor was frigid. The steaming soup on the table before him did nothing to warm William. Neither had the fire built in his chambers.

Why did the damnable Eaton family have to live on the outskirts of a village so far from everything and everyone? At least his ancestors had the decency to build Hockley Castle in the center of the East Midlands.

Trent Castle was an absurd name since the Eatons lived in a stately two-hundred-year-old home with a faux turret. The building did not even possess a dungeon or a moat. To reach its non-existent curtain he had trudged through the city, the countryside, and the village. He had frozen his balls off while the winter precipitation turned his nose into an icicle. And, now, the dowager's lifted chin and puckered lips made the dining room colder than the rare blizzard outside.

If angry huffs contained fire, then Alistair Eaton could have heated the large room from his seat at the foot of the table. His brow furrowed as he gulped from his wine glass. "Astleyshire—"

The proper old woman gawped at her oldest grandson.

Alistair sighed. "Your Grace, please forgive Lady Georgiana's absence. My sister is not feeling well."

William's plan was almost on track. He had done his research and all evidence indicated that Winkentattle was an educated man, living near Trent. One credible source reported that Evan Eaton recently left Trent Castle in the middle of the night and was seen conversing with a known Luddite.

He did not give two shites about the libelous rubbish distributed on flimsy folded paper. However, he gave ten million fucks about Evan accusing him of cheating. He may have been a womanizing rogue, and he occasionally drank too much. But he never cheated.

His friend had issued an invitation for him to stay and time with the Eatons would afford him time with the fiery hellcat.

Chaperone his bloody arse. Courting her was out of the question, not that she would be interested. Although, he had never met a woman he could not entice to crawl beneath him. Still, the money and the women meant nothing; he hated to lose a wager.

Three birds dead with one stone. The first throw, winning his wager. The second, granting the favor the Prince Regent had asked of him by exposing Winkentattle. And the ball-tingling bonus, destroying Evan Eaton in the process.

A pink tornado whirled into the room. "Please forgive me. I was lighting the Yule log in the drawing room and accidentally dropped my pearls into the fire."

The supposed sick Lady Georgiana seemed quite healthy despite her slovenly appearance. Even though long red strands of hair stuck out in every direction, her exquisite gown was rumpled, and black smudges covered her cheeks, the strand of pearls above the appealing swell of her bosom remained pristine.

The dowager countess brought a hand to her heart and gasped. "Georgiana! We were to light that after dinner."

Alistair emitted one of his huffs as his younger brother chuckled.

The disheveled woman looked William in the eyes and her breath hitched. Of course, he did cut a fine figure in his burgundy cravat and double-breasted waistcoat.

And the rumor was she hated men? Blimey lies. He held in his chuckle as he shot her his lopsided grin, the one that turned women into molten heat.

Her nose crinkled, her face contorted until she resembled a gargoyle, and she *ack*ed at him as if she smelled a rat-infested sewer. "*Bah,*" she added before falling into an ungraceful curtsey. "Your Grace."

He would swallow a lot to achieve his mission, but he would not pretend to be a dolt or suffer insults from an unlady-like chit.

"Lady Georgiana, I am glad to see you are healthy. What a miracle that your pearls remain exceptionally white while the rest of you looks like you have been sweeping chimneys." He tossed her back his best shit-sack grin.

Georgiana's lips formed a straight line, her eyes narrowed, and her cheeks turned a brilliant crimson. He braced himself for her rebuke. However, the tight-jawed dowager commandeered the moment.

"Please excuse us, Your Grace. 'Tis most urgent that I consult with Lady Georgiana about her illness and make sure the log was lit correctly. We certainly do not want bad luck for the New Year." The countess folded her napkin, placed it on her plate, stood, and grasped Georgiana's elbow.

"Ouch!" Lady Georgiana glared at the fingers gripping her. "Who said I was unwell?"

The dowager nudged the chit out of the room, whispering, "Confounding young ladies should not play in dirty hearths."

Interesting. Leaving the dinner table? And in the presence of a duke. Although he was the one who had insisted that they pretend he was not there.

During the ensuing silence, he schemed. Perhaps he would put the situation out there and gauge Evan's reaction. "Alistair, tell me, how are your tenants faring this holiday with the food shortages and the unrest in the factories?"

The earl worked his jaw from side to side. "The countess is determined to hold a Twelfth Night Ball. It will be the first one at Trent Castle in over two decades. She is sparing no expense. And Georgiana planned the annual Trent Castle party this evening."

That was not what William had asked, and how ironic that servers took that moment to lay out decadent trays of oysters and loaves of fresh bread with sweet black butter.

"Our Georgie has made the best of the situation and has put together generous charity boxes for many of the struggling families," Evan said. "She may be a bit wild. But she has a huge heart."

"I do not know that *wild* is the correct word," said Alistair. "Free-spirited is a better description."

The girl was one step away from being a feral cat. Was the earl so desperate to marry his sister off that he would lie? Perhaps all of the Eatons, including his dear friend, were untruthful bastards.

"Have you read the stories that Winkentattle is distributing?" William asked. "It seems they are quite scandalous. The working class outwit the aristocracy and upper class at every turn. The author seems to think he is that fictional hero Ned Ludd."

Alistair stuck a fork into an oyster and blanched. His wine, on the other hand, seemed to go down smoothly.

Suspicious! Perhaps, the actions of a man who knew of his brother's traitorous accusations against the Crown?

"The Frame-Breaking Act is non-negotiable, punishable by death. Did you know that thirty men were tried for the uprisings near Cleckheaton?" William ran the side of his hand across his neck. "Execution." He grinned. What a splendid job he had done researching these past two weeks.

Alistair's pallor resembled a decaying olive. "I am not sure what these *Tattle's Tales* have to do with factory uprisings. To my knowledge, no machinery has been broken."

"They are causing unrest with the working class. Making them think they deserve more wages and fewer hours. This is how the violent protests started in every instance." William cut his gaze to Evan. "Have you read anything this Winkentattle has written?"

Evan shrugged. "I understand Parliament's take on

this. However, I have my opinion."

"Evan," Alistair grumbled between clenched teeth.

William forced his friendly smile. "Alistair, we are among friends. I would love to hear…" As his heart dropped to his stomach, he pushed back the internal warning: *William, spying does not agree with you.* He picked up his glass and sipped.

"Originally, the Luddites may have intended to halt progress," Evan said as he forked an oyster.

"Go on," William said.

"At first, the skilled craftsmen were replaced with unskilled labor that could run the machines. Many were women and children. Now they work long hours with no breaks. The landed gentry are becoming wealthy while their workers can barely afford food. Some even live on the streets."

After waving to a server, Alistair held up his empty glass.

"I find Handershane to be an absolute arse," Evan said. "He owns the lace factory in our village."

"I believe he was recently appointed a baron," William said.

"Yes," said Evan. "Dishonest and appointed to Parliament. And for some god-forsaken reason, he has the prince regent wrapped around his finger."

Even though he agreed with the assessment of the newly appointed baron, William held his tongue.

"Although the machines are cost-efficient, they are hardly safe. Four weeks ago, a child crawled into one to fix a blade and had his arm crushed." Evan looked up from his oysters. "The arm became infected and had to be amputated. The injured boy was only twelve. And two weeks before that, four children were left orphans.

After their father died of consumption, their mother took his job. She died when her skirt caught fire on a dick pot."

Orphans? For Christ's sake. How low would this Ned Ludd-want-to-be sink to rabble rouse? "Simply stories. 'Tis my understanding that weavers earn more than farmers."

"That is not one of Winkentattle's stories. The man who died was our head groomsman's nephew," Evan said. "And just look at the poor weavers. Their skin is bleached from the long days spent indoors, and many have lung disease from the poor ventilation."

"Nonsense." William was not gullible. "That is propaganda." On second thought, despite his research, perhaps he had no idea what he was talking about.

An emerald dream gracefully entered the room. The only thing remaining of her earlier appearance was the strand of pearls around her neck. Her cheeks had been scrubbed until they shone, and her hair was pulled into a neat coiffure with a single soft curl hanging past her *décolletage*. Was it possible that the swell of her breasts was even more tantalizing?

There was no sign of her previous anger, and her smirk had morphed into a frown. And her eyes. My God. He hadn't noticed them before, but they were the same shade as the gown.

The countess followed behind her, looking as if a long stick had been wedged into her buttocks. If William didn't know better, he would think there was a dueling pistol aimed at the rebellious girl's head. Why else the smug expression on the older woman and the change in the demeanor of the younger?

The women sat and resumed the soup, which by

now had to be as cold as the grand room they occupied.

"Why, Georgie, you look quite handsome," Evan said.

"Lovely," Alistair said.

Stunning! Except her smile was so forced that William experienced sympathy pain in his jaw.

Lamb chops smelling of mint, glazed ham, a rich potato and spinach blend, and artfully arranged fried cauliflower were carried to the table on silver platters.

Except for the occasional clink of a glass, the room was quiet as Alistair carved the ham.

Instead of waiting to be served, Georgiana pushed her brother's hand away, stabbing and shuffling through the slices, until she found the largest chunks. "Were you discussing Winkentattle before we entered?"

"I do not think he is appropriate dinner conversation," the countess said.

William was about to request they discuss the topic anyway when Georgiana opened her mouth to say something, looked at her grandmother, and clamped her lips tight. Her facial muscles twitched while she added two lamb chops to her plate. Wait. Was the chit, peering at him from the corner of her eye?

From beside him, the countess's voice faded in and out as she spoke about the Christmas Eve preparations.

Perhaps his brain was frozen, the wine was strong, or he was tired because William found the redhead shoveling meat into her mouth akin to an aphrodisiac. His cock twitched and he tried to shake off the unwanted haze. It was no use.

Discombobulated, he blurted out, "Alistair, my brother and sister have other plans, so I will spend my holiday fortnight at Trent Castle."

Where in the bloody hell had that come from? One week was bad enough and now he had invited himself for fourteen days.

How dreadfully awkward that the Eaton family wore wide-eyed expressions as if they had just witnessed a Christmas hanging.

He picked up his drink, chugged, and then held the glass high, bobbing it up and down. He needed a refill—and quickly.

****

"Damn!" William stabbed a poker into the burning log. "Damn! Damn!"

What had he been thinking? Now he would have to send his valet for more clothes.

William had not lied when he said his family had other plans. His sister was in Paris studying with a master art instructor and his brother was traveling Italy.

He did not mind being on his own for a few weeks. And the last thing he wanted was to be with the Eaton family. Alistair, his old friend, was palatable—maybe a bit uptight, but he did have his hands full. However, strangling Evan before he had proof that he was Winkentattle, was a good bet. The countess's terrifying demeanor made him want to confess to crimes he had not committed. And Georgiana Eaton. Well, the woman was infuriating. Beautiful but infuriating. William knew she was difficult so why was her dismissal so irksome? What did it matter that she had kicked his ego all the way to hell? And, why, at six-and-twenty, did his damn prick still have a mind of its own?

Pouting alone in his room was not his style. He would search out Alistair for a drink. Or maybe he would track down Evan and challenge him to a game of cards. The man had a serious tell. He sucked his jaw when he was lying his arse off. William should ply him full of whiskey, rid him of the coin in his pocket, and get him to confess to his crimes. All the while, the louse would suck on that damnable jaw.

Or maybe he would track down the redhead. He would corner her somewhere, stare into her eyes, finger a lock of that brilliant hair, and vex her with snide remarks.

She would stick out her bottom lip, and her cream-colored cheeks would turn an endearing red. Thereupon, he would pepper her with flirtatious innuendo. Yes. Antagonizing Georgiana Eaton would be a hellishly fun way to pass Christmas Eve. Reject him, his arse. Before the night was over, she would ache for him.

Chuckling, he set the poker beside the fireplace and pulled his chamber door closed behind him.

Chapter Four

Christmas Eve, December 24th, 1816

"Ah, ha." Goldcount recalled the half-eaten sausage in his breeches. He pulled it out, tossed it to the hungry canines, and then waddled across the field as fast as his stubby legs could move.
From Tattle's Tales

Hands on hips, finger waggling, the Eatons' head housekeeper, Mrs. Teague, scowled up at Georgie. "The countess will not be happy that you are up there. What if you fall and get hurt?"

"I have told her the same thing, Mrs. Teague. She simply refuses to listen." Millie cocked her head to the side. "*Hmm,*" she murmured. "Make the bow bigger."

"Lady Georgiana inherited her stubborn streak from her father," declared Mrs. Teague.

"Or mayhap her grandmother."

Since she was often the cause of others' consternation, Georgie held her tongue. Instead, she concentrated on tying the mistletoe into place with large loops. Taking care to place her flimsy shoes on the center of each step, she descended the ladder and then sprung to the middle of the drawing room to eye their handiwork.

Boughs of evergreen and hawthorn festooned the

stone fireplace and chandelier. Red velvet ribbons held sprigs of holly, delicate paper flowers, and red and green apples in place, and a candle burned on each of the window ledges.

Her most precious display was the two-foot evergreen tree she had placed on a table in the center of the room. She had tied little red bows on each of the branches and placed wrapped packages for her family at its base.

Since it was hard for her to sit still, it had taken her months to embroider simple monogrammed handkerchiefs for her brothers. The picture of Trent Castle that she had crafted for the countess looked as though a child had painted it and her grandmother would probably want to throw it into the rubbish bin. Still, she had tried to make something lovely.

Georgie popped onto her toes and clapped. "It looks lovely."

"Indeed, it does, Lady Georgiana," conceded a now smiling Mrs. Teague. "Maybe next year we should get one taller than the earl. Maybe it might even become a fashionable trend."

Georgie fashionable? Never!

"I wish I had someone to kiss beneath the mistletoe." Millie stared at the bunch hanging from a medallion in the center of the room as she wore that faraway dreamy look that made Georgie want to box her ears. "So, tell us about dinner. What was His Grace like?" Millie asked.

Georgie sighed. "He is like every other clueless aristocrat." A smirking, blue-eyed, aristocrat.

"You are an aristocrat," said Millie.

Georgie rolled her eyes.

"When you get to be my age, you truly appreciate the fine jaw and broad chest of a man. And the duke is quite the specimen," said the normally proper Mrs. Teague.

Georgie *harrumph*ed.

"Oh, Mrs. Teague," Millie said, "if the countess heard you say such things."

"So true," Mrs. Teague said. "So true."

"But he is handsome, isn't he?" Millie said.

The two women giggled.

Georgie crinkled her nose in disgust. Perhaps her grandmother was correct the millions of times she declared their household staff was too familiar.

The door opened, Evan strolled into the room, and his eyes brightened. "It looks fabulous." He waved off the staff as they fell into curtsies and *Master Evan'd* him to death.

"It is the prettiest display in years." Taking in every detail, Georgie spun in a circle. The decorations complemented the forest green and dusty rose upholstery and rugs. "How does the dining parlor look?"

"Every needle is in its place. Her Lady Pain-in-the-Arse would have it no other way." Evan looked above him at the "kissing" bough made of mistletoe and apples. He grinned, then winked at the petite blonde lady's maid.

Millie's cheeks turned crimson and her gaze dropped to her feet as Georgie jabbed an elbow into her flirtatious brother.

Evan rubbed out the sting and chuckled. "Why am I the recipient of your violence? It should be the other way around. Grandmother hasn't stopped complaining about you lighting the Yule log without us."

Georgie cringed and pointed to the hunk of tree against the far wall. "Do you want to help me light it now?"

"Why, Lady Georgiana Eaton, you untruthful charlatan." Evan doubled over in laughter.

"What in the dickens are you two talking about?" Mrs. Teague asked.

"One wonders how our delicate lady managed to cover herself in soot before dinner. And while wearing such a lovely frock," Evan said.

"Bugger off," Georgie said.

"Oh, Lady Georgiana, you didn't? We worked so hard to make you presentable," Millie said.

After Alistair's shocking declaration, she had been left with no other choice. No duke worth his dukedom would want to court a filthy woman. However, she had not expected his sideway glances to heat her to the very core. She waved her hand in front of her face to cool her cheeks.

"I wondered why you changed gowns without me," Millie said.

"I accidentally dropped my pearls into the fire in my chamber," Georgie said, even though she had visited one of the unused guest rooms and wallowed in a dusty hearth.

Millie scowled and tapped her foot while Mrs. Teague threw her hands in the air.

"Come on, Georgie," her brother said. "Help me heave this thing into the fire before Alistair discovers you are sabotaging his attempts to marry you off to His High and Mighty."

Evan puffed up his chest and imitated the duke's

swagger as he strolled across the room. Not that Evan didn't have a similar I-am-king-of-the-world-gait.

"Lady Georgiana will ruin her dress," Mrs. Teague said. "Millie, you help Master Evan."

"I will be careful." Lowering her voice, Georgie impersonated the duke's husky lilt. "*Nonsense, that is propaganda.*" She pulled her shoulders back and strutted across the room. Once she reached the log, she knocked Evan out of the way and plunked herself down in the middle. "I win."

"Am I interrupting?" asked a deep baritone from the doorway.

Millie and Mrs. Teague fell into curtsies.

Evan grumbled under his breath and cleared his throat. "Georgie and I were racing. An Eaton tradition. 'Tis good luck to sit on the Yule log before you burn it."

Holding her breath, Georgie looked over her shoulder at the powerful presence filling the doorway.

Singeing her corneas with his sapphire-colored eyes, the duke strolled into the room. "I thought Lady Georgiana already lit the Yule log."

So what if he knew she had lied? Perhaps he would get the hint, and realize she had no desire to know him. Wait. She did not want to know him, did she? Hell no. He needed to return to Hockley Castle.

"We burn two Yule logs at Trent Castle," Evan said.

Foiled. Now Georgie had to play along unless she wanted to make her brother out to be a lying scoundrel.

"Yes, two," she said so quietly she could barely hear her own voice.

"My lady, my lord, Mrs. Teague, Your Grace."

Jimmy Clayton stood in the doorway with his arms folded. Looking quite self-conscious, he tucked the stub attached to his left elbow under his right arm.

No one pointed out that the sweet boy had addressed them in the wrong order.

"The gingerbread and syllabub are ready for us in the dining parlor," Jimmy said.

Cinnamon, nutmeg, and cream.

"*Mmm*." Georgie salivated.

"To the parlor," sang Evan with a raised fist. "We will meet you all there. Georgie, help me toss this thing into the fire."

The staff filed out the door, chattering away. Georgie hopped off the log and prepared to lift her end.

The duke's eyes were so wide that they resembled Damson plums. "Let me." He attempted to step in front of Georgie.

Evan choked back a laugh.

"I beg your pardon." When she pushed the duke to the side, the mere second's touch left her breathless. She gasped and checked herself. She would not succumb to being a ninny. Scooting low, she tucked green velvet between her knees, and hefted. Seconds later, flames consumed the log.

Georgie swiped her hands together to brush off the dirt, then smoothed her unblemished skirt. "Perfect!" She stepped around the gawping man and headed for the door.

Evan followed.

"Lady Georgiana," William Harrington called after her.

She cringed, then faced him. Firelight illuminated stunning eyes and dappled over thick, dark hair.

"Mayhap I could escort you to the parlor," he said.

So that he could ruin her evening by ensconcing her in his many different smirks? There was the puffy lipped one. The crooked smile to the left. The lip down on the right. The slow spreader. The twinkle in the eye with the lip bite... Good Lord. He must practice them in the mirror.

"I'm sure you can find your way. And if not, Evan is an excellent guide," she said.

Turning her back to the men, she feigned a nonchalance she didn't feel. Firstly, if her grandmother got wind of her rude behavior, she would renege on her promise to get Georgie that puppy.

And secondly, William Harrington the Second smelled of tantalizing citrus and cedar and stood beneath her mistletoe.

Chapter Five

Christmas Eve, December 24th, 1816

The bed creaked and the mattress sagged beneath the baron. But he did so love sleeping with his gold.
From Tattle's Tales

Damn Thomas Merrick and his bloody wager!

Why in the hell was he furious? Since he did not want to court Georgiana Eaton, and he had Evan Eaton's undivided attention, his plan was almost going perfectly.

Still, who did the confounding woman think she was? Being disinterested in men was one thing, flat out rudeness was another. Besides, all women adored him; not one had ever turned him down. Perhaps slamming Evan against the wall and smashing his whirlygigs up his arse would relieve some fury.

"Come on." Evan motioned for him to follow.

William hesitated for a second before catching up to the back biter.

"Forgive Georgie," Evan said. "She grew up with a family of men and has never quite embraced feminine nuances."

She better damn well develop some quickly since she looked like a woman and oozed passion.

"Once she cut off all of her hair and showed up at

our private fencing lessons. She stole my clothes and shoes since I was the youngest and Father almost sent her away. But after she outmaneuvered Stephen and me both, he let her stay. Although, he did eventually make her grow her hair back." Evan slapped William on the shoulder and chuckled. "Duke, do not annoy her near something sharp."

William's sister was partial to her needlepoint and art lessons, as were most women he knew. Georgiana Eaton was not just infuriating, she was also fascinating.

"And the countess's presence has us all on edge. Our grandmother means well, but she feels we have lacked a strong female presence for the past two decades. Mrs. Teague mothers us, and Cook treats us like her grandchildren. But still…" Evan shook his head. "Well, we are a bit spoiled and unruly, leaving Alistair with his work cut out for him."

William fought his urge to say, *Hear, hear.* "Alistair has changed from our school days."

Of course, inheriting a title and responsibilities had also turned William from a carefree rogue into a parcel of twisted nerves.

"I fear the poor chap will be gray and wrinkled within the year. I must also confess that we are worried about our brother. He has not yet returned from France."

"He was quite the hero at Waterloo," William said.

Evan's chest lifted. But only for a moment. Then his pride left him with a *woosh.* "Hopefully, our grandmother won't swoon when she has to sit beside a groomsman?"

"What?" William asked as the men navigated a galley of portraits.

"She hits the floor with even a hint of impropriety and another of our traditions is that everyone at Trent Castle celebrates Christmas Eve together. From scullery maid to earl."

"Interesting," William murmured.

"My mother held the first gathering almost thirty years ago, and Georgie ensures that we carry on in her memory. 'Tis actually quite fun."

As they descended the main staircase, resplendent with fresh greenery, the smell of citrusy pine permeated the air. "That boy—what happened to his arm?"

"Jimmy?" Evan asked.

"Is that the boy who was just in the drawing room with us?"

"Aye. Great lad. That is Jimmy Clayton. Cook's youngest grandchild. He cut off his arm so the working class could spew propaganda."

What in the hell did that mean? Perhaps an uppercut to his jaw would knock Evan Eaton out cold.

William unclenched the fist hanging beside his thigh and shook out his fingers. Even before his ducal responsibilities hung about him like a necklace of cast iron cannonballs, he had worked hard to put his fighting days behind him. Besides, all gazes were on Evan and him as they strolled into the room.

In less than two hours, the cold dining area had been transformed to a festive party and at least four dozen people milled about the room. Like the drawing room and stairwell, a plethora of evergreens, red bows, paper flowers, and apples adorned the great room. Candles flickered in every window, creating an illusion of warmth despite the snowy night outside the castle walls. Trays of gingerbread, miniature cakes loaded with currants, biscuits, and sugared pears filled the table.

Jimmy scooped a creamy liquid from blue Delft china. Alistair and the older Lady Eaton chattered with the white-haired butler. Georgiana Eaton and three maids stood near the fire.

For the first time, William witnessed Lady Georgiana's sincere smile and it pummeled him in the stomach.

Her cheeks were pink, and the firelight brought out the golden highlights in her red hair. When she looked his way, her lips turned down at the corners, and her skin bloomed crimson. Her gaze dropped to the floor briefly. Then, pulling her shoulders back, she returned her attention to her companions.

He wanted nothing more than to stand near that fire with her by his side as he watched the rise and fall of her perfectly pale bosom. He ran a tongue over his top lip.

"*Hmm*," his companion murmured.

Bloody hell. Had Evan just caught him fantasizing about the chit?

Perhaps not, because Evan inclined his chin to the boy they had just been discussing. Jimmy Clayton balanced the cup on his stump, picked up a plate, then headed toward William and Evan. He stepped carefully, watching the punch all the while.

"Your Grace, Grandmum says you are the guest of honor. Would you like some? 'Tis made of brandy and cream." The cup lifted a fraction of an inch.

"Take it, Astleyshire," Evan said.

William accepted the offered treats. "You are a fine server," he said, in all sincerity.

The care the boy had taken not to spill a drop was impressive as hell.

"Thank you, Your Grace. But I want to be a physician someday."

Grinning, Evan ruffled the boy's hair. "Dream big, my boy. Dream big!"

From the armless grandson of a cook to a physician? Probably not, although deep in his heart, William hoped that the boy defied his class and handicap.

"Hello, Merry Christmas," someone called from the entranceway.

Three soldiers in the red uniforms of the 1st Life Guards stepped forward.

Lady Georgiana sprinted across the room, then leaped into one of the men's outstretched arms. Her feet lifted from the floor and her skirts swished as he spun her in a circle. Her giggles found their way to William's core.

What the hell? The man had the same green eyes and red hair as the woman warming his cheeks with her palms and wore the three stars and red coat of a captain.

Within moments the three visitors held drinks and plates of food and had become the focus of the gathering.

"How lovely. We will have quite the ensemble for Christmas day." When the dowager countess smiled, she wasn't nearly as intimidating. "I will have rooms prepared for you all."

"Your hospitality is most appreciated, but we will quarter with our men," said the distinguished-looking man wearing the crown insignia of a major.

"We can put your regiment up in the old chapel.

'Tis not being used right now," Alistair said.

"We will have the fire started and Cook can send a warm meal right away," said the countess.

Georgie brushed a finger across the captain's cherry-colored nose. "You look dreadfully tired, and you are frozen to the bones."

William could not identify the foreign sensation rendering him addle-brained. He wanted to stomp across the room and pull Georgiana Eaton from the man's grasp.

Instead, he made his regrets and retraced his steps to his chamber.

He threw open his door, slamming it behind him. He tramped to his mirror, tugged off his cravat, and grumbled to his reflection, "Merry Bloody Christmas, you damn fool."

It seemed he had been unwittingly infected with a severe case of redheaditis. The bloody symptoms included inane jealousy, pangs in the chest cavity, and a hard-as-stone prick.

He groaned. Add stupidity to the afflictions. He hadn't seen him in a few years, but the captain in her arms had to be Georgiana's twin, the heroic Stephen Eaton.

Hell and damnation. The chit turned him inside out.

Chapter Six

Christmas Day, December 25th, 1816

Maria Seraphina grabbed the sturdy vine and swung across the Trent River. She landed in front of the baron. "If you even look at Jackson Valiant with your beady eyes, I shall remove them from their sockets."
From Tattle's Tales

Georgie awoke Christmas morning with a warm heart. The fire crackled and she snuggled under her blankets. If only she had a puppy to cuddle with.

"Don't be so spoiled," she whispered.

One of her wishes had come true. Stephen had three days' leave, so it would be the best Christmas ever. Well, as long as her grandmother was not too unbearable, it would be the perfect holiday. Hopefully, entertaining their visitors would occupy the cranky countess.

However, if William Harrington did not keep his distance and tried to court her, it would ruin everything. His sapphire-blue eyes and thick, black lashes added to the problem. And, oh, that arrogant grin.

The previous evening, she had been convinced he would walk across the parlor and talk to her as she visited with the maids. And she had wanted him to. So much so that her toes had tingled. Shoving her face into the pillow beside her, she muffled her absurd whimpers.

Toe tingles? Preposterous.

Her chamber door creaked. "Merry Christmas."

The door clicked into place.

"Are you feeling well?"

"Bollocks." Caught behaving like a simpering fool, and over a man. Georgie peeked out from under the pillow and deflected. "Merry Christmas, Millie. I shall go with you tonight to meet Christopher." She pushed herself to sit and leaned against the headboard.

"My lady…Miss Georgiana…Georgie… But with so many visitors you will be seen."

"Not if I am in my disguise."

Millie pulled the draperies wide. When she faced Georgie, the light shining into the room settled into her creased brow. "That sounds dangerous with the soldiers here."

"Not at all. They are on Christmas leave, and I will be unrecognizable."

Millie's nose crinkled so much that she could have been smelling a chamber pot.

"Do you think we will be able to get to church this morning?" Georgie asked.

"Yes. The men have been working since dawn to clear a path to the village."

"Why did you not wake me to help?"

Millie *tsk*ed, sat on the end of the bed, then grasped Georgie's hand. "I know how you feel about the Duke of Astleyshire. But consider what marriage to him could do for your causes. You might even gain an audience with the queen." Millie held her hand to her heart. "And he is so handsome."

Georgie groaned. The man was devilishly good-looking.

"I know he was a scoundrel in his youth, but they say he has matured since inheriting the dukedom. And the way he looks at you…"

Firstly, how much maturation could a man undergo in two months? And secondly, he had gawped at her like she was a filthy rodent when she appeared at dinner covered in grime. That was precisely what she had wanted, so why did his grimace hurt her heart? Although that was nothing compared to how his twisted grin indicating he knew that she had played in dirt on purpose made her feel.

"He cannot take his eyes off you," Millie said.

Something fluttered in Georgie's chest and her gaze fell to her lap. "Because I am making such a spectacle of myself. Millie, I truly do not want to court or marry. I would have to leave Jimmy, Cook, Mrs. Teague, and my brothers. A husband might not allow me to read and write and fence."

Georgie shuddered at the thought of a man crawling on top of her to plant his seed. Or maybe it was a pleasurable shiver? Whatever it was, it was foreign and unsettling.

"I will go with you to Hockley Castle, and you will make new friends. 'Tis not that far. You can come back and visit."

"But 'tis not as wonderful as Trent Castle." At least she suspected that to be the case since her home was the most incredible place in the world. Georgie exhaled frustration as she crawled out from beneath her warm covers. "I should like to wear my royal blue dress to breakfast and church."

Millie rubbed her hands together. "Splendid. You

look lovely in that gown." Her lady's maid skipped to the wardrobe.

"Millie, whatever shall we do about your silly notions?"

"Lieutenant Calhoun is also quite handsome, and he is taken with you."

Millie may have been beyond help when it came to romance, but she was perceptive. Stephen's young second lieutenant had tracked every one of Georgie's movements the previous evening. The man was gentlemanly and heroic and had once helped Stephen save their company from an ambush.

On second thought, perhaps she should have chosen the orange dress with red flowers. It clashed with her hair making her resemble a glowing lobster.

Millie cradled the blue dress as if it were her lover. She waltzed arm in arm with it until she reached Georgie's side.

Although she adored breakfast in the parlor with her brothers, Georgie opened her mouth, intending to ask for a tray to be brought to her room. All of the male attention left her on edge. And, if William Harrington were not in the same room with her, they would not have to spend time together. She did not have time for this toe-tingling and chest-fluttering nonsense.

However, there might be honey cakes. She clamped her lips tight as Millie fussed over her.

****

Georgie entered the parlor to a round of Merry Christmases. Seven men and a smiling dowager were seated at the table. She beamed at her brothers, acknowledged Major Blythe and Second Lieutenant Calhoun, and ignored the duke, her gaze settling on a middle-aged, balding man with the jowls of a hound dog.

How dare the man sit at their breakfast table.

"Georgiana, do you remember Sir Gerold Handershane? Handershane, my sister, Lady Georgiana," said Alistair.

There was no need for introductions. They knew each other well since Georgie had once defended herself against his inappropriate leering with a finger flick to his bulbous nose.

"'Tis Christmas morning, and you find yourself at our table instead of with your wife and children? Does anyone else wonder why?" Georgie asked.

Her grandmother brought a hand to her heart and gasped. Someone choked—probably Alistair. Georgie turned her back to the wide-eyed party and busied herself at the sideboard in search of the largest honey cake.

So what if she had been rude? The man had earned his title and wealth by working the townspeople to death. He was responsible for Jimmy's injury. And if the rumors were true, he often visited a brothel and took *the drip* home to his poor wife.

Georgie had just plunked a spoonful of eggs beside her cake when the memory of her promised puppy hit her with a brutal punch. The dowager's nasally twang echoed between her ears: *If you behave like a lady in the duke's presence, I will make sure that you have the pick of the litter.* Surely being polite to the Duke of Astleyshire and the scandalous Baron Handershane were not the same. She should have broken her fast alone in her chambers.

The informal seating arrangement allowed her to

squeeze in between Stephen and Evan. Sitting across from her, the blond Benjamin Calhoun studied her full plate and grinned.

Since the man was a war hero, she smiled back as she retrieved the cup of hot tea the countess sent in her direction. Typically, her appetite matched her brothers, but the conversation rumbling from every direction soured her stomach. She set her fork down and rubbed at the ache in her chest.

Her grandmother sat between the distinguished, graying Reginald Blythe and William Harrington, and the baron had made himself cozy on the other side of the duke.

When Handershane leaned into the duke's space and chortled, he flashed everyone a mouthful of chewed-up food. William cringed and then chuckled. However, Georgie would bet her beloved honey cake that his laugh was forced.

William Harrington lifted his tea to his lips. His gaze pinned on Georgie, he blew on the steam rising from the cup.

Her cheeks grew hot. Perhaps from her own warm drink. "Your Grace," she called across the table.

The chatter surrounding them stopped.

Were his blue eyes as cold as an Arctic iceberg or as warm as the summer sky? Or did they contain the power of the ocean?

"Yes, Lady Georgiana?" he asked in a voice so deep her torso vibrated.

The damnable orbs froze, singed, and slapped at her as if they were a tidal wave.

"One wonders what you and your dining partner find so amusing," she said.

"Things unfit for the feminine ear," said Handershane around a mouthful of pork.

"My Grace, do you find coarse conversation appropriate while seated beside the countess?" Georgie asked the duke, even though she could give two farthings about the propriety of breakfast discourse.

Her grandmother's raised eyebrow was a warning that she should cease calling insults down the table at once.

Suddenly William Harrington's lids drooped, giving him a rather appealing sleepy look. "There should never be a coarse conversation when a lady sits at the table."

His heavy-lidded eyes, along with the dropping intonations of his voice, tickled Georgie between her thighs. The almost imperceptible nod he tossed in her direction seemed to promise, *But when not at the dinner table, he can say wonderfully filthy things.*

Where in the blazes had that come from? She must be coming down with an illness because she wasn't thinking straight. If a man ever said untoward things to her, she would knock him on his arse.

"If you wish to speak about such things, mayhap you should spend Christmas Day with your own families and leave mine to enjoy the holiday with some decorum."

Obviously, the beastly men were not with their families because they were…beastly!

Handershane chortled. "Lady Georgiana and decorum? Now that would be something to see." He slapped the duke on the back and shoveled more pork into his snout.

Georgie attempted to stand, but Stephen held her in

place. Meanwhile, her grandmother poured water into William Harrington's teacup. He grasped it between large hands and blew on the steam.

Why did the aristocratic man have the forearms of a laborer?

How unfair. She had taken the time to dress, so he should be forced to roll his sleeves down like a proper gentleman.

"Major, how are your men faring? Are they warm? Well fed?" the countess asked.

"Your hospitality is most appreciated," Major Blythe said.

"Let us talk about Christmas dinner," the countess announced as breezy as if there were no awkward discomfort at her table. "Your men will have goose, mincemeat pies, and cider. As for the family, we should balance out the number of females. It will keep everyone on their best behavior—"

Georgie tuned out her chattering grandmother. Unfortunately, Benjamin, who couldn't have been more than ten-and-eight peeked at her every few seconds. Her gaze traveled past her grandmother and landed on the duke. Her cheeks again absorbed heat, but this time it couldn't be her tea since her cup was empty.

William Harrington's lips parted as his tongue darted out to lick away a crumb of cake. Then the fool grinned at her. This was a new grin, twisted and devilish, almost as if he knew every one of her secrets.

"Major Blythe, I am so glad that His Royal Highness had the foresight to send help. After this rabble-rouser reads his story, there could be backlash at my factory," Handershane said. "This Winkentattle needs to be strung up by his balls in the village square."

Georgie shook off the intoxicating haze that William Harrington blew in her direction and focused her attention on the major as he said, "Hopefully, there are no issues."

From beside her, Stephen stiffened. Then the reality of the situation hit her.

She grasped her twin's hand. "Are you home because you have been stationed in Trent to keep the factory workers from protesting about their working conditions?"

"Yes," Stephen said. "But I am able to spend my holiday leave with my family and then our men are to report to London." His normally genuine smile was so forced it split Georgie's heart in two.

"But you were the bravest squadron fighting Napoleon," Georgie said. "Why would you be sent here?" How naive of her to think that she could keep those in power from finding out about her public reading.

Alistair groaned.

"Large gatherings lead to protests, and protests often lead to violence," Major Blythe said. "And there have been recent outbreaks from Yorkshire to Derbyshire."

"I'll say it again. Hang Winkentattle the trouble-making bastard up by his balls," announced the uncouth Handershane.

Evan sent Handershane a look filled with shrapnel. "Negotiations about safer machinery resulted in management scoffing. Work stoppage led to more unskilled laborers and hungry children being brought in. Requests to have families of the injured and deceased compensated met with deaf ears. Although, how can one compensate for a young boy with no arm and the children left orphans? The only thing left seems to be an act bound to gain attention: camaraderie amongst the downtrodden."

When had Evan educated himself about something other than cards and women?

William Harrington locked his gaze with Evan's. The smirking duke lifted his teacup in the air as if toasting some kind of battle.

Meanwhile, the countess continued to chatter on and on about something or other.

Georgie stood. "We should leave for church. We want to get good seats."

It was an absurd declaration since the Eatons and the Beaumonts always occupied the front row. And a duke would be treated as if he were the king himself.

The truth was Georgie needed to pray. Immediately.

The protest she had sparked was about to put her twin in harm's way.

Chapter Seven

Christmas Day, December 25th, 1816

A smiling Maria Seraphina sheathed the knife and tucked it into her garters.
From Tattle's Tales

Of course the despicable man's wife and babes were in London for the holiday. Who could blame them? And if Handershane elbowed William one more time, the buffoon would find himself knocked flat on the church floor. It was not as if William did not enjoy taking in the attractive women, but they were in church, for blazes' sake.

Following Handershane's reverberating whack to William's shoulder, he quietly excused himself to seek a private moment in the church garden outside a side entrance. Once he was alone, he exhaled, and his frustration mixed with the icy condensation, floating upward in curling wisps. Snow-coated shrubs lined the walkway, and the majestic steeple rose into a vibrant blue sky.

"Father, I wish I had one more Christmas with you," William said.

"Your Grace. Your Grace."

Lady Beaumont and her two daughters strolled toward him, then fell into curtsies.

He never could remember the damn girls' names. However, the eldest, with her big blue eyes, was lovely. Her blonde hair glistened in the late morning sun, and she was long-limbed and lean. However, unlike most beautiful women, her smile left him unimpressed.

"Your Grace, do you remember my daughters, Arabella and Rose?"

"Of course, how lovely to see you again," William said.

"The countess has invited us to dine with you this evening." Lady Beaumont fluttered her lashes.

Arabella sashayed into his space and also fluttered hers.

Bloody hell. Now was not the time to fend off husband-seeking mothers and their flirtatious daughters.

"The Eatons are delightful hosts," he said.

"Surely, but poor Louisa…" Lady Beaumont leaned close and whispered, "Alistair and Stephen will make wonderful husbands. Evan may never be more than a handsome rogue, but he is charming. However, that granddaughter of hers…" The gossipy woman shuddered.

Poor Viscount Beaumont.

Seeming to delight in her mother's horror, Arabella smirked as her thin neck bobbled like a chicken looking for feed.

At least Georgiana Eaton was not an addle-brained social climber; she was a brilliant firebrand. "Is the service over?" he asked.

"How our vicar does talk." Lady Beaumont's chortle emanated from deep in her throat and burst from her as if she were a braying donkey.

"Your Grace," said the youngest daughter, whose

voice was less affected than he predicted. "I think it has just ended." She swung her hand toward the crowd filling the front walkway.

"Please forgive me. I should find the Eatons," William said.

Miss Arabella boldly placed her hand on his forearm just as Lady Georgiana glided underneath a trellis. The redhead's expression was dreamy as she smiled at a blue tit merrily chirping.

William forgot to breathe.

When Georgiana looked up and noticed the four of them, she frowned. Her gaze met William's, and a blush that matched her hair overtook her cheeks.

"Lady Georgiana," Lady Beaumont called, with a superficial wave.

Georgiana bit her lip, turned on her heel, and headed in the opposite direction.

"Please excuse me." William brushed away Miss Arabella's hand. "Lady Georgiana."

Although she halted, her back remained to him. She only stood still for a moment before she skittered away.

He extended his stride and caught up to her. "My lady, may I walk with you?"

She shrugged. "I would prefer you walk at least seven fathoms behind me."

He flung his arm in front of her, forcing her to stop. "You, Lady Georgiana, are exceedingly infuriating and vexing."

"And you, Your Grace, are an arrogant jackass." She shoved his arm out of her way and lifted her skirts. "Stephen, Alistair, wait up." She hurried toward her brothers.

Using the tip of his boot, William kicked snow into the air before trudging after the siblings.

Within seconds, Handershane waddled alongside him, chattering incessantly. This was insanity. Helping his cousin was not worth having to spend time with the boorish prig.

Georgiana strolled between Stephen and the damn second lieutenant. Alistair, Major Blythe, and Louisa Eaton led their train. A handful of servants trailed behind the group. Since Evan Eaton was nowhere to be seen, he was undoubtedly up to no good.

When Lady Georgiana turned her head to say something to the frigging Benjamin, she smiled. William groaned.

Meanwhile, Handershane blabbed. "I proclaim that protesters should be shot on sight, and if anyone destroys the looms, they should be flogged in the village square."

Shootings? Floggings? What in the hell had he gotten himself into?

Lady Georgiana skipped from the men, bent forward to retrieve something from the snow, then stood. She flung her arm forward. A snowball smashed into the heroic Stephen's face. Chortles contorted her body as she clutched her ribs.

Stephen packed, then tossed a snowball at his sister's back as she trudged into the snow.

William stopped in his tracks.

Despite wearing a gown and velvet pelisse, the woman navigated the knee-high accumulation as if it were nothing. She sought safety behind a tree and taunted her brother with another snowball barrage.

From out of nowhere, Evan flew to his sister's side.

Soon the two of them pelted a laughing Stephen.

The countess, Alistair, and Major Blythe faced the battling trio and watched with wide-eyed wonder.

"*Aurugh,*" came Evan's battle cry. "Get Alistair!"

Georgiana pitched the snowball that smacked the earl's nose. He brushed white powder from his face with an indignant *harumph.* Tightly packed balls hit him on each cheek. His brothers chortled, and Alistair sprinted to a fence post.

"Children," yelled the countess as she clapped her gloved hands.

Her reprimand was pointless because the adult Eaton siblings were in an all-out war and snowballs flew from every direction.

A renegade shot from Georgiana hit the second lieutenant. It was all of the encouragement the soldier required. He formed a weapon of his own and chased after the giggling lady.

"Everyone, get Alistair," Stephen yelled.

Following the command, Alistair became the target of every hurled item.

William could contain himself no longer. Tossing proprietary to the wayside, he joined the game and raced to Alistair's side.

"Now, you will be conquered," hollered Alistair. "Harrington and I will reign supreme."

The teams had been chosen and territory was established. Icy snow pummeled William as he packed his weapons and fought the gleeful enemy.

In the confusion of battle, he somehow came face to face with Georgiana Eaton, her hair blowing, her cheeks glowing. Paralyzed by the most beautiful woman he had ever seen, he was left defenseless. A snowball smacked him in the face. She bounced from one foot to the other, wound up, and hit him again.

Adrenaline took over William's spirited play as he charged. Together, they tumbled to the ground.

What the hell had he done?

From beneath him, Georgiana wriggled. Then in one swift move, she rolled him onto his back, straddled him, and shoved handfuls of snow into his face. It was a good thing it was nippy since his body heated with both humiliation and a raw, aching need.

"Bloody hell," someone yelled.

Lady Georgiana crawled off him, leaving him arse down in a drift. He cringed because any second, three angry brothers would tear him limb from limb. He would allow Alistair to shoot him between the eyes if it came to a duel.

Expecting to be surrounded by furious Eatons and the finest soldiers, he sat up. However, no one was paying attention to him because they surrounded the dowager.

She lay in a motionless heap.

Chapter Eight

Christmas Day, December 25th, 1816

"All for me. All for me," sang Baron Goldcount as he sat alone and feasted on one hundred roasted Christmas geese.
From Tattle's Tales

Georgie held the steaming tea to her cheek and inhaled. The warm cup and the roaring fire in the drawing room hearth annihilated the bone-cold chill she had caught during the winter trek and icy battle. Her gaze landed on the mistletoe, and another surge of heat shot through her.

What would it be like to kiss a man beneath the magical greenery? And what if that man were the Duke of Astleyshire? Would he caress her face and be gentle? Or would he pull her to him and press his muscular body to hers?

Despite the heat, she shivered. At one-and-twenty, she had not yet desired to kiss any man. The aggravating William Harrington would not make her mawkish. She eliminated him from her thoughts with a vigorous full-body shake.

The dowager's satin skirt swished as she entered and crossed the room to sit on the settee beside Georgie.

"Are you feeling better, Grandmother?" Georgie asked.

The countess fingered the silver case hanging about her neck. "Since coming here, I must carry my pomander with me everywhere. I have no idea what to do with the lot of you. What a display. And in front of Major Blythe, the staff, and the duke."

Blaming her grandchildren for her swooning spells was absurd. "You could just loosen your stays," Georgie said.

"Oh, my." The countess sniffed her container, then retrieved a fan from the side table and fluttered ivory and feathers back and forth in front of her flushed face.

"We were just having a bit of harmless fun," Stephen said from the doorway.

He and Alistair strode across the room to take turns kissing their grandmother's red cheeks.

"I am sorry to have caused you distress. But I assure you, Major Blythe took no offense, and Astleyshire got caught up in the fun himself," Stephen said.

The countess *tsk*ed. "And you, Alistair? You are an earl."

"Even earls should occasionally have fun," Georgie said.

Stephen patted Alistair on the shoulder. "It was good to see you happy."

"I am sorry, Grandmother. But I confess, I loved feeling like we were children again. Even if it was only for a few moments." Alistair smiled as he plopped himself into one of the fireside chairs and crossed his booted foot over his thigh.

"I do hope that none of you misbehave at dinner in

front of the Beaumonts. Sylvia Beaumont would love nothing better than to badmouth us to the *ton*," said the countess.

Georgie snorted. "Then why would you invite them?"

"The Beaumonts? Oh no. Keep our fair Georgie away from the punch bowl." A grinning Evan strolled across the room, his higher-than-usual collar giving him an elegant appearance.

Despite her scowling grandmother, Georgie laughed at his comment.

Evan squeezed in between Georgie and the countess, and with her family surrounding her, all felt almost right with the world. Luckily, the horrific Handershane had returned to his home, alleviating one of the stresses in Georgie's life. She simply needed to keep her thoughts off of both her upcoming reading and the Beaumonts' visit.

Oh, and William Harrington's lips. She should definitely not think about that smirk she wanted to kiss away. Wait. Kiss was the wrong word. Slap away.

Eventually, Benjamin and Major Blythe joined the Eatons. Hands clasped behind his back, the major stood at the window, his attention split between the view and the gathering.

Benjamin sat across from Georgie, occasionally peeking at her and grinning. The soldier would make a doting husband for a woman seeking a heroic, pleasant man. Georgie was not that person.

A festive feeling blanketed the room as Georgie and the countess poured tea and everyone chatted—everyone but the duke. He was nowhere to be seen. Which was just fine with Georgie since she was not thinking about him, or the way her heart had sped up when he lay on top of her hours before, his breath tickling her cheek.

Unfortunately, the spell was broken when Chester, their beloved butler, hobbled into the room, rang a bell, and announced, "Lord Trent, the Viscount and Viscountess Beaumont have arrived."

Double bollocks.

"Alistair, do watch out for Miss Arabella. She has designs on marriage," Evan said. "It seems her Season ended with a ruined frock instead of a proposal." He winked at Georgie.

Georgie rubbed at her chest. Arabella infiltrating Trent Castle? Over her dead body. Although, if it was not for the punch debacle, the woman might be happily engaged and not chasing after the Eaton siblings.

Hmm? Maybe she should try to be less impulsive.

Lawks! Her grandmother might be brainwashing her, the same way she muddled Alistair's thoughts before sucking the joy from him.

"Aye, and you be careful of Miss Arabella, brother. Especially with your breeches that tight and that collar swallowing your face," Alistair whispered back, his emerald eyes glittering.

"Evan, I dare say, you make the perfect tulip," Stephen said.

His palm facing him, Evan formed a V with his middle and index fingers. "Bugger off, the both of you."

Normally Evan dressed more like a sporty Corinthian than a fashionable "pink of the *ton*," and their conversation was not even the slightest bit humorous, so why were her brothers chuckling? It must be a man thing, and unfortunately, Georgie had the misfortune of being born a woman.

Her grandmother sat so straight she was lucky her head didn't poke a hole in the castle ceiling. "Chester, please show them up."

Chester nodded and his ancient body attempted a bow. "Yes, my lady. And Cook says Christmas dinner is ready."

"We are waiting on His Grace," the countess said.

Evan *harrumph*ed and sat forward. "After his display with our Georgie, the bastard should pack his bags."

"Or marry Georgiana." Alistair leaned back in the chair and pinned Georgie in his gaze. "If only he could come to know her so that he could officially propose."

Benjamin's tea halted halfway to his mouth as he met Georgie's gaze.

Alistair relaxed? Evan on edge? It was all too confusing. Georgie's face heated at the many gazes cast in her direction.

"Why was I not told that he plans to propose to my twin?" Stephen asked.

"*Shh.*" Georgie held her finger to her lip and inclined her chin to the major, whose back faced them.

"They have been to hell and back with Stephen and are now family," Alistair said.

When the major turned to face them, the countess blasted him with one of her rare smiles.

"Because our sister is doing her damndest to sabotage his courting her," Alistair said.

The countess's smile morphed into a frown. "Georgiana?"

Georgie's foot tapped the floor as if she was

smashing an ant colony. "Do not talk about me as if I am not sitting in the room." And in front of the company! What had gotten into her family?

"That man is up to something. I can feel it." Evan crossed his arms over his chest. "I do not trust him or Handershane."

Alistair cleared his throat and opened his mouth to say something when a commotion in the doorway distracted him.

Mother and daughters tried to come through the door together. They did not quite fit, so the viscountess rearranged them by knocking Rose to the side. Lord Beaumont trailed behind his family. His face, eyes, and the wispy patches of hair sticking out of his scalp were all grayer than ashes. His soul and passion? Dead.

In complete contrast to her father, Arabella was a rainbow of colors. For a lean woman, her cleavage was impressive. She made a lovely picture with her big eyes and golden hair.

Every man in the room stood and did a double take.

In comparison, Rose looked plain. It was as if a bluebird followed a peacock. What did that make Georgie? A pigeon? A red-headed freckled-faced pigeon.

Lady Beaumont swished to the countess, bent forward, and kissed her on the cheek. "My dear Louisa, do not stand. I know how your fainting spells do plague you. And how lovely the castle looks with all of the homespun decorations. We had arrangements made in London for Wayside House. Red and white hothouse roses as big as Lord Beaumont's head and the most divine greenery."

The dowager's knuckles turned white as she

clutched the teapot. She set it on the table, wiped her hands on her skirt, and smiled. "That sounds delightful, Sylvia. You have always had marvelous taste. I hope to visit and see for myself. I do love roses."

Lady Beaumont eyed the garland above the fireplace and cringed. "Yes. Roses are sophisticated."

The simpering Arabella's gaze followed her mother's as she stretched her giraffe-like neck into the rafters and blanched.

"I like our apples and fresh greenery," Georgie said.

"They are fine for now," Lady Beaumont said. "But for the Twelfth Night ball, you should consider something a bit more fashionable."

All chatter stopped when William Harrington swaggered into the room. His red velvet frockcoat tapered in at his waist, and his cravat was a matching shade of luxurious silk.

The Beaumont females fell into curtsies as they "*Your Grace*d" him, and her austere grandmother let out a sigh filled with girly affection.

"Pardon my tardiness," the duke said, with a gentlemanly bend at the waist. "I sent my valet for clothing more suitable for our joyous celebration and the path from Hockley Castle proved challenging due to almost impassable roads. He only just arrived."

Evan leaned close to whisper into Georgie's ear, "His Arse is just embarrassed to show his face."

Normally she chuckled at Evan's observations, but since the duke didn't seem embarrassed in the least, Georgie frowned. How could William Harrington ooze confidence after pressing his hard muscular body against hers? His face should be as red as his fine clothing. Or at least match her scorching cheeks.

Within seconds, the Beaumonts surrounded the duke. Arabella Beaumont did not have designs on Alistair Eaton, Trent Castle, or the Eaton's estates. Nay, nay.

Her focus was one hundred percent on the duke standing beneath Georgie's mistletoe.

Chapter Nine

Christmas Day, December 25th, 1816

Goldcount struggled to button his velvet coat. But attending the opera alone was indeed a fine way to spend Christmas.
From Tattle's Tales

While linking arms with the elder Lady Trent and escorting her down the grand staircase, William discovered the woman was not nearly as unpleasant as he initially thought. In some ways, she reminded him of his late grandmother.

"Please forgive a poor hostess for her inadequacies," Lady Louisa said.

On the other hand, Lady Beaumont was a lacey nightmare, and her cutting remarks directed at their hostess boiled William's blood.

"Louisa, you are a fine hostess and I am having a delightful holiday. Pay no mind to Sylvia Beaumont," he said.

"I am afraid my grandchildren have grown wild and the staff too familiar. My husband, God rest his soul, my son, and my daughter-in-law all left this world too soon. My son was not much older than Alistair when he inherited an earldom. I think his heartbreak ultimately wore him down, and his struggles meant he gave into his children's every whim." A few tears dripped down Louisa's cheeks and her gloved finger dabbed them away. "I miss them all so much. And I love and want the best for my grandchildren."

Within seconds the watery-eyed woman was again emotionless stoicism. However, the quick glimpse into her heart endeared her to William.

He patted her forearm. "Alistair was the finest of my friends at Bedford and Cambridge. I am of the opinion that Stephen has the courage of a lion times ten." And he found lying on top of Georgiana Eaton in the snow to be the greatest of aphrodisiacs. However, he would see Evan Eaton hang. He looked away from the dowager's green eyes that were so much like her granddaughter's, composed himself, then faced her. "I find you a pleasant hostess, indeed."

"My granddaughter was born into this world with more energy and wit than is acceptable for a lady in genteel society. Rather than change her, I would prefer the *ton* accept her. But people like the Beaumonts will never see her positive attributes."

Unfortunately, the countess spoke the truth, because no lady liked to feel inferior to another. And no man wanted to have to match intellect with the fairer sex. However, he doubted Georgiana Eaton gave a farthing about the *ton*, and damn, that was appealing.

"Mayhap if you are kind and gentle and give her babies, it will temper her wild side," Louisa said.

Kind and gentle? Babies? Not him. He was just trying to bed her and win a wager. Some other man would marry and tame Georgiana Eaton.

Once they reached the table, William pulled out the countess's chair.

"Georgiana may end up a lonely spinster. I have not a doubt she believes this is what she wants. But—" The countess shook her head before lowering herself onto her seat. "I do not want her to be lonely and without family. Heed an old woman. The elderly become invisible."

"You, my lady, are far from elderly or invisible." William patted her hand affectionately before sitting at the head of the table.

He inhaled the aromas of roast beef, goose, Yorkshire pudding, baked yams, and potatoes. Licking his lips he said, "Now, this is a Christmas feast."

Louisa Eaton seemed to forget Sylvia Beaumont's cuts because she beamed.

Soon their party was seated, a matriarchal sentry on either side of William. From the other end of the table, the gregarious Eaton siblings engaged in lively conversation. Roaring with laughter, Georgiana threw her head back, and her bosom bounced with each chortle. When she caught him gawping, he lifted his chin in acknowledgment and grinned.

So much for his attempts to flirt. She scowled and slammed her fork down with so much force the nearby dishes vibrated.

Sylvia Beaumont leaned close to whisper, "That girl lacks refinement. Now, look at my Arabella."

Arabella brought a bite of yam to her mouth and nibbled.

Georgiana picked up her fork, shoveled in a bite of roast beef with gusto, and his balls tightened.

A half dozen gazes landed on him. Christ. Had he moaned?

How long had it been since he had bedded a

woman? He would have lain with Lady Hemmingworth a fortnight ago if he had not lost himself in his cups. Unfortunately, he had gotten so foxed he had passed out beside the widow's luscious body before satisfying himself.

Servers carried festive candles, mincemeat pies, and flaming cups of plum pudding to the table. Raucous applause broke out from the Eatons. William appreciated their enthusiasm so much that he clapped and hollered an enthusiastic, "Whoo, whoo."

Georgiana Eaton peeked at him from the corner of her eye. She looked away quickly and her cheeks turned crimson.

"*Mmm.*"

What would kissing her plump breasts do if she flushed that much from a glance? Her nipples were probably rose pink against her pale skin.

Damn! He needed a woman. He gulped his brandy and used the back of his hand to dry his mouth.

Arabella Beaumont caught his gaze, fluttered her lashes, and smiled.

Although husband-seeking, mean females were not his type, she was a woman. He smiled back just as Georgiana Eaton again peered at him.

Flutter, flutter went Miss Arabella's lashes. He chuckled and tipped his empty glass to her. Lady Georgiana frowned and stabbed at her food.

Was the unreachable Georgiana Eaton jealous of Arabella Beaumont?

While the diners dug into their plum pudding in search of the prized coin, he sought Georgiana Eaton's attention, then shifted his gaze to wink in Arabella Beaumont's direction. From his peripheral, Georgiana folded her arms across her chest and scrunched up her freckled nose.

How absolutely, deliciously fun.

He clutched his bottom lip between his teeth and let his gaze travel over Georgiana before settling on Arabella.

Arabella twirled a strand of hair around her finger and pulled her shoulders back. Despite the lady's beauty, he found her as appealing as a fly-covered corpse. Now, Georgiana Eaton made his cock stand at attention.

The second lieutenant lifted the elusive coin into the air, proclaiming himself the winner. Georgiana shifted her attention to the smiling man.

William was beginning to dislike the soldier almost as much as he disliked Evan. He forced out a fake, "Hurrah, Benjamin," that mingled with the rest of the congratulations, then dug into his currants, sugar, and cream.

Once the dessert dishes were emptied, the countess cleared her throat, announcing that the women would be retiring to the drawing room. Alistair invited all of the gentlemen to his study.

First, to beat the jaw-sucking Evan Eaton in a game of cards.

Then he would track down Georgiana Eaton in a dark corner and kiss her senseless.

Chapter Ten

Christmas Day, December 25th, 1816

Jackson Valiant used the point of his sword to flip Baron Goldcount's pink feathered cap into the mud.
From Tattle's Tales

Although Georgie wanted to join her brothers in their spirited card game, she excused herself. Grumbling, she took the stairs two at a time.

The ridiculous Beaumonts were gone, and although sweet and handsome, Benjamin Calhoun needed to lavish his attention on someone that was not Georgie. Then there was William Harrington, and his blue eyes and bloody smirk. If only she were a man. Then she could challenge him to a duel. She would back him into a corner and… She moaned.

At least Major Blythe, with his distinguished graying temples and regal jawline, kept her grandmother occupied.

Perhaps fear about the reading sparking protests were the cause of her disquiet. She would tell Christopher to halt preparations immediately.

She was almost to her chambers when William Harrington stepped out of the shadows. Momentum propelled her forward and she crashed into his imposing figure.

His strong hands clasped her waist, both steadying her and singeing her skin through layers of fabric. "Lady Georgiana, where are you off to in such a hurry?"

As if it were any of his business. "It was a busy day, and I am quite tired."

Still holding on to her, he quirked an eyebrow. "You, my lady, have the energy of a honeybee."

"Excuse me." She attempted to push past him.

A muscular thigh lunged in front of her. "Did you receive your Christmas wishes?"

His seductive voice made her wish for strange things. Whispered secrets. Caresses. Stolen kisses in dark stairwells.

Instead of a furry bundle of joy, she had a soldier that followed her around like a lovesick puppy and an arrogant duke who lurked in every corner and stared at her as if he were a wolf.

"No."

She stomped past him, threw her chamber door open, slammed it behind her, then leaned her back against the frame as she tried to catch her breath.

****

Thirty minutes later, Georgie wore Evan's old wool greatcoat and worn-out buckskins. Millie helped to tuck her hair under a top hat. A pair of boots from her brother's youth completed the disguise. If Georgie and Millie linked arms and hurried through the dark, they might be mistaken for a young couple engaged in a clandestine affair.

Millie made sure the hall was clear before the two of them tiptoed down the servant's stairwell and crept into the cold night. Unfortunately, the icy trail proved too treacherous for horses, so they undertook the path on foot.

Georgie carried a servant's lantern containing burning rushes. Luckily, the wind carried away the unpleasant smokey odor. With her free hand, she held her hat in place as the wind whipped at her face. Millie's cloak and skirts lifted with each blustery gust.

By the time they stood beneath the colorful sign of a gentleman riding his horse, they were chilled to the bone. They bypassed a dozen drunk men and climbed the narrow stairwell to the third floor of Sampson's Tavern.

Georgie knocked. Seconds later, Christopher ushered them into a small meeting room.

Two men Georgie had never met sat in front of the blazing fire. One was the size of a giant, the other grew a beard that hung to his chest. They greeted Millie, then relinquished their hearthside seats.

Neat piles of the holiday edition of *Tattle's Tales* sat on a dilapidated table. Never having seen a stack of her writing before, Georgie exhaled a long slow breath of contradicting emotions.

"This is Lady Georgiana Eaton," Millie said.

Christopher stepped back and looked Georgie over.

First, she removed her wet gloves. Thereupon, her hat and a few strands of hair tumbled to her shoulders.

"My lady," Christopher said, with a bend at the waist.

"Please do not." Two days ago, she would have grinned and said, you mean Winkentattle. Instead, she frowned. "Call me Georgie." She held her frozen fingers near the fire, praying for a quick thaw.

"Of course," Christopher said. "I did not recognize

you. Your disguise is better than the last time, but you do not quite look like a lad yet. Try a wig instead of a cap."

The other men mumbled their agreement.

"You took quite a risk coming this evening without our escort," Christopher said.

Although the men folded their bodies into their newly chosen seats, their postures remained rigid.

"We have everything arranged. Tomorrow eve you will appear at the Boxing Day celebration in the square in your disguise and read the holiday installment of *Tattle's Tales*. At the stroke of midnight, forty able-bodied men will break down the factory door, smash windows, and destroy the looms. Five men in masks will converge on Handershane in his home and threaten him. There is no way he can continue to ignore our demands if he feels vulnerable. Any arrests will be met with villagers ready to loot and burn." Christopher chuckled manically. "We will outnumber the parish constabulary, a village to three."

Georgie rubbed her temple. "We need to call off my appearance and the protest."

The man farthest from Georgie sat forward, his massive body threatening to break the legs of the too-small chair. "Everything has been arranged."

"I did not predict that soldiers would be sent to stop us. I want to bring attention to the unsafe conditions. I do not want people to die." Perhaps even her twin.

"Soldiers?" The large man clenched his jaw. He leaned back in his creaking chair. "No disrespect, my lady, but we can handle a group of pampered king's guards."

"These men are the finest of His Majesty's soldiers," Georgie said. "They were responsible for Napoleon's defeat."

The large man huffed. "Christopher, I told you not to let an aristocrat, especially a woman, become the figurehead for our movement."

The bearded man said, "We did not know she was wealthy and naive when we read the first story."

Damnation. So, she was naive? His intense gaze sliced through skin and bone to pierce her soul.

"We will continue with our mission, with or without you, my lady."

Georgie rallied and stiffened. "Do not forget that my stories are the reason the surrounding villages support your efforts. 'Tis their numbers that will provide your cover."

"Christopher," Millie said, her voice and eyes pleading, "Young Jimmy, and Oliver's nieces and nephews, all left orphans…and so many others. No one should die needlessly."

Christopher's eyes softened and his brow furrowed.

The large man drummed his fingers on the chair's arm. "Why would the lard-arsed prince pull troops from France to send to our humble village?"

"I would guess to make an example of us, Peter," Christopher said. "And apparently, *Tattle's Tales* have reached the *ton*, and some find the stories sensational. Rumor is the batty king is not so mad that he can be bamboozled into paying his son's debts. Since the prince has a mistress who requires excessive amounts of fabric and lace, he made Handershane a baron."

"They are a lot of gluttonous fools," Peter said. "We will continue with our plan."

"No." Georgie held up a palm. "I have an idea. Winkentattle will be indisposed and unable to make the reading. I will write a new story leaving Goldcount out. Instead, Jackson and Maria will enjoy giving to others for the holiday. In four days, we will get word to the villagers that the true holiday tale will be read by Winkentattle in the town center." She would do whatever was needed to ensure Stephen would be safe and out of the way.

Peter snorted.

"Christopher," Millie said, "please."

Christopher stood. With his hands clasped behind his back, he paced. Finally, he stilled and faced them. "Tomorrow night Winkentattle's fake tale will be distributed." He pointed at Georgie. "One page so that we can waive the half-penny price and give it for free. We do not need riots because the villagers feel betrayed by Winkentattle. Three nights from now, Winkentattle reads the holiday story. We attack the factory and Handershane in his home."

There was no way they would hang an entire village, so why did Georgie's heart drop to her feet? And why was it so difficult to breathe?

And were three nights enough time for Stephen to be safely on his way?

Chapter Eleven

Christmas Day, December 25th, 1816

The baron chortled as bacon grease dribbled down his chin. He had Jackson Valiant by the balls. Or so he thought.
From Tattle's Tales

Ale dribbled down the grizzled man's chin. He finished chugging, slammed his mug on the bar, and clapped William on the back. "We're garn ter get that bloody bastard tomorra'."

William wiped the stranger's saliva from his cheek. "Which of the bloody bastards 're we garn ter get?"

The disheveled man's head bobbed about as he focused on William's face.

Thank deuces William had asked his valet to bring an old suit of clothing since it would not due to swagger into the village tavern wearing his new custom tailored topcoat.

"Handers-shane," the man slurred.

At least the drunk hadn't said the Duke of Astleyshire.

In a desperate attempt to avoid a case of the chilblains, William finished his second cup of ale and requested a third, all the while keeping his gaze on the stairwell. What in tarnation was taking Evan so long?

The arse was probably poking whomever he had left Trent Castle with. He would bet his stale ale that it was one of the scullery maids.

William had fought his curiosity and kept his distance as he followed them. Once, he had slipped. He caught himself before falling, but his boots had crunched in the snow. The cold air absorbed the sound, and the pair continued their trek without looking back.

Three jug-bitten men elbowing each other in jest now blocked his view of the stairwell. Meanwhile, his foxed companion rambled on—some nonsense about a fistfight he had once won.

Perhaps, the girl was a cover, and Evan was meeting with his fellow rabble-rousers. William needed to investigate.

"Is there a room upstairs?" he asked the tall bloke behind the bar. "I might need a place to lay my head."

"Got no rooms tonight," the tavernkeep said. "But Cleo's six doors down can put ya up if you are willin' to empty yer pockets."

The man seated beside William chuckled until he choked. "There ye have the added amusement of a doxy. You like 'em fair? Dark? Cleo's got 'em all."

William stayed far away from brothels. His preferences lay more toward bored countesses and widowed duchesses. Although, a feisty redhead seemed to be his current flavor of the day.

Damn. He needed to wash that chit away with a drink. He guzzled, then held his mug high, waving it at the tavernkeep.

"I used to be a weaver," his drinking companion said. "A damn fine one too. But they replaced me with a machine and a dozen lads straight from their mother's teat."

"That there is a crime," William said in his best rustic voice as he gulped his fourth mug. "But yer could clean up and get yerself a new job."

The man burped. "Aye. Now I muck the s-swine s-stalls at S-sparrow Farm." He pulled his shoulder back, lifted his nose in the air, pursed his lips, and moved his shoulders back and forth. "For His Grace, the bloomin' dashin' Duke of Astleys-shire."

William's mug halted halfway to his mouth. First of all, he was tired of people imitating him. He did not walk like he had a stick up his arse or thrust his shoulders about like a frigging fool. And secondly, Sparrow Farms was one of his properties. "What are you doing here in Trent?"

"Me daughter and grandbabes is here in Trent, and it was the only job I could get. And after I lost me job, the bas-stard baron raised our rent. Almost twice as much."

William guzzled as he formed his question. "Does the duke treat you well?"

"The late duke was a rat bastard and this one ain't much better. No idear what is going on with his land or how hard his farmhands is workin'."

That dudgeon both stung and bit. "The late duke was a bastard?"

"Where have you been? Sittin' in alehouses in your fancy threads swillin' bud?"

William dropped his gaze to his chest and lap. Fancy? The entire night had been a ball-freezing waste of time. Was he sitting there listening to some old drunk insult him and his family, or would he climb those stairs and catch Evan up to no good?

The drunk nudged his shoulder. "Wanna hear a secret?"

William did not want to spend another second in the man's presence. He stood.

"Ye might find this interestin'. Its-s about Handers-shane."

"Go ahead," William said.

"After the prince made 'em a baron, he started chargin' his highness-ss-s's *modiste* four times what he's chargin' others for lace."

Although not surprised by the double-cross, William asked, "How do you know this?"

The man aimed for his eye but tapped his nose. "I seen the receipts with me own eyes. Plus, I got one in me pocket. Stole it while the baron was shinin' 'is own willy and kept it in case I ever needed it."

The baron shone his willy where other people could witness it? William gagged.

The man produced the receipt and grinned proudly. "He's-s a bloody bastard."

William scanned the paper. "Can I have this?"

"No."

"I will pay you."

Just as William reached into his pocket, a commotion broke out. A man wearing a top hat plowed through the customers and out the door.

One of the drunks made a fist. "Come back here, ye Merry Andrew!" He stumbled about as he punched the air.

Georgiana Eaton's ladies' maid stood in the doorway. She looked over her shoulder at someone in the stairwell, smiled, pulled the hood of her cloak up, and fled into the night.

William slammed two shillings on the bar, tossed coins to the old man, and grabbed the receipt, grumbling, "Merry Christmas." Thereupon he followed Evan and Millie.

****

William kept to the shadows and tucked into an alleyway. His vision blurred and his head spun. He was one hell of a spy—half-foxed and pining for some woman who had sworn off men and despised him. And what in the blazes for? To prove to his late father, who was apparently a *bas-stard* that he would make a good duke? To seek revenge on someone who had accused him of cheating? To win a paltry bet?

Enough was enough. In the morning he would pack his things and return to Hockley Castle.

He followed the pair a few more feet and halted. Cleo's establishment appeared like a beacon in a storm. The light emanating through the lattice windows beckoned and taunted. The couple in front of him became ever smaller as they scampered away. The brick and stucco building housing women, ale, and a warm fire was so close.

Patrons had worn a trail through the snow, making the more scandalous path an easier trek. He stepped onto the cobblestones leading to sweet lips and luscious breasts. What could one night of debauchery hurt? It was Christmas, after all, and he deserved some sort of pleasure.

"Your Grace," someone behind him said.

Hell and damnation. Identified in front of a brothel.

He slowly pivoted as a small figure stepped into a ray of moonlight. "Your Grace, are you ill?" the child asked.

Shock knocked William from addle-brained to lucid. He attempted to straighten his body, and spoke slowly, enunciating his words.

"Jimmy, what are you doing out at this time of night? 'Tis dangerous in this part of the village."

"Aye, 'tis, Your Grace. Are you protecting them too?" Jimmy pointed his stump at the lantern disappearing into the night.

What? A half-frozen one-armed boy protecting Evan Eaton and Lady Georgiana's maid?

"I always look out for the Eatons," Jimmy said. "His lordship is getting me a puppy. Georgie is learning me my letters and numbers so I can be a doctor. Evan is teaching me to fence like a one-armed pirate. And Captain Eaton is the bravest man in the world."

Even in the dark, William knew the shivering boy's chest puffed with pride. Although the brave Jimmy was the most loyal of servants, he was still a child.

"Let us get you home," William said.

The boy fell into step beside him. "Everyone thinks the countess is cross, but she sneaks me sweetmeats when Grandmum isn't looking."

William chuckled. "I am not surprised."

The pinch-faced dowager was a sweetheart under all that frowning anxiety.

"You won't tell?" Jimmy asked.

"Your secret is safe with me, young man."

They exited the village and headed into the woods where the snowball fight had taken place. The memory of Georgiana beneath him warmed William's blood.

"I've been thinking of naming my pup Duke. Is that disrespectful because I don't want Grandmum or the countess to be angry?"

As they strolled side-by-side, William rested his hand on Jimmy's shoulder. "I should be most honored to have your dog named after me."

"Your Grace, did you get your Christmas wishes?"

William had asked Georgiana that same question just hours before and her answer had been a resounding *No*.

"Jimmy, do you know what Lady Georgiana wished for this Christmas?"

"Well," Jimmy said. "She asked his lordship for a herder, too. Then our puppies can play together. But…"

"But what?".

"I overheard the countess say Georgie cannot have the pup unless she treats you with respect."

"Is that so?"

Jimmy shrugged. "Millie says Georgie is just being disrespectful because she is confused by your blue eyes."

How utterly delicious.

In the dark, he could not make out anything but a faint silhouette and the sincerity in the boy's words. "Girls are pretty, but they get confused over the oddest things."

"Indeed." William chuckled.

Forget leaving in the morning. The unreachable Georgiana Eaton had an Achilles's heel, and William planned to use this newfound knowledge to his advantage.

"I hear one-armed pirates can take on an entire fleet using their wits," William told the lad as they headed toward the castle.

"Your Grace, can I tell you a secret?"

If he counted finding out that his blue eyes

confused Georgiana Eaton, that meant three secrets in one night. He chuckled. "Most assuredly."

"I cannot tell Lord Trent or Master Evan because I do not want them to be sent away for killing the baron. But I don't think you could kill anyone."

William halted. What had the repulsive Handershane done?

"There is this pretty girl. She is ten-and-eight and she was my friend at the factory."

William's stomach roiled as he listened to Jimmy confide secrets no young boy should have to keep. The lad was wrong about one thing. William was capable of violent murder.

Just put one perverted prick and a sword in front of him, and there would be bloodshed.

Chapter Twelve

Boxing Day, December 26th, 1816

Maria Seraphina flew in on her vine and opened the prison door. Jackson Valiant grinned at his rescuer.
"I think a certain baron may wish for visitors this evening," he said.
From Tattle's Tales

Despite her late night, Georgie awoke before dawn on Boxing Day. Instead of taking their much-deserved day off, Millie and Jimmy insisted on helping her deliver packages of jams, dried fruits, and cakes to a dozen families in the village. The road had thawed enough for the horses, so Georgie drove the curricle with Millie by her side as Jimmy perched in the small rear seat. The fresh air cleansed her lungs and the sun rays glistened on the snow-peaked mountains in the distance, energizing her.

Later that morning, Georgie hummed as she arranged wrapped packages under the tabletop tree. There were colorful hair ribbons for Millie, soft winter gloves for Mrs. Teague and Cook, and pencils and paper for Jimmy. Hopefully, Chester could tell that she had embroidered a CH on his handkerchief. Oliver, the head groomsman, had a special place in Georgie's heart since he had taught her to ride, so she wrote him a joyful poem about galloping through the country. Finally, there were wool socks and shiny coins for the entire staff.

Georgie spent the early afternoon writing her new story. With pencil and paper in hand, she paced from one end of her room to the other, only standing still long enough to scribble about the benevolence of her hero and heroine. She spent the late afternoon imitating a male voice as she read to her reflection in the mirror.

Even though she congratulated herself for her backup plan and new tale, Georgie's food soured in her stomach.

Jimmy had helped circulate a story to the soldiers that Winkentattle would not be appearing, and a special free story would be distributed. Once Stephen was on his way to London and safe—she sighed—*not* safe, but at least she would not be responsible for any danger he encountered, Winkentattle would appear. Hopefully, the real holiday tale was so exciting that when she read it, Winkentattle would be forgiven for his canceled appearance.

It was late afternoon when she flitted through the castle, aching to hug her twin and hold him close to her heart.

He was not in his chamber, Alistair's study, the library, the drawing room, or the great room. Unfortunately, none of her brothers seemed to be about. If they had left her behind to run off and do something exciting, she would never forgive them. And, if anything unspeakable had happened to Stephen, she would never forgive herself.

Since most of the staff were gone for the day, the house was quiet. While heading to the garden for fresh air, exuberant cheers startled her. She halted before the ballroom to place her ear against the thick wood. Claps echoed.

That could only mean one thing—and how dare they!

She pushed her weight against the heavy door and plowed into the massive room.

A group of men stood against the far wall watching as a foil fell from Evan's grasp and clattered against the ballroom floor. Stephen retrieved the weapon and handed it to Evan. Her brothers continued fighting until the point of Stephen's blade touched Evan's shoulder. Major Blythe, acting as the official, declared the winner. A mixture of applause and jeers broke out as Evan congratulated Stephen.

Fencing at the Eaton's home was akin to illegal bare-knuckle fighting, where both shouting and coarse language were accepted. Good thing, since Georgie hated having to pay two pence every time she dropped a *bloody hell.* As usual, protective masks lay unused in passive defiance of both etiquette and safety.

Frowning, she made her way to the men.

"Hello, Lady Georgiana," Benjamin said.

"Good day, Lady Georgie," Jimmy said.

She glowered at Alistair. "Why did you not include me?"

Her oldest brother looked at his feet. "Because we have company."

"And Grandmother would slice off his balls," Stephen said.

Evan covered his crotch with his weapon-free hand. "You would have three ball-less brothers."

Alistair cringed and all of the men chortled.

"Do you fence, Lady Georgiana?" Benjamin asked.

"Our sister is a damn fine swordswoman," Stephen said. "As well as a respectable pugilist. Gave me more than my fair share of bloody noses."

Why was William Harrington snorting?

Paper and equipment littered the ground. Georgie navigated the clutter to squat beside a mesh mask holding folded slips. She used a nearby pencil to scribble *GE* on a blank square and tossed her entry into the mask.

Benjamin Calhoun gasped.

"Surely you jest," William said.

This was precisely why a lady should abandon stays. She never knew when she would have to kick off her silly slippers and show a man up.

She placed a hand on her hip. "Since I did not know that I needed to bring my pin money, one of my brothers needs to lend me coin."

"But you are in girl clothes," Jimmy said.

She hefted the back of her day dress to the front and grasped the seam. Using all of her strength, she tore the fabric, creating a slit. How embarrassing that her task required a lot of huffing and puffing instead of one smooth rip.

"Rules?" she asked.

Alistair sighed—long and loud. "One crown to enter. The first one to administer three touches wins. The winner of each bout pulls the name of his competitor from the kitty. Benjamin beat Jimmy. Jimmy did exceptionally well, but I won that round."

"His lordship paid my share, and I will work it off," declared Jimmy, his grin so big his cheeks puffed up.

Alistair ruffled the boy's hair. "In the next bout, Evan cheated and beat me."

Evan's middle and index fingers formed a lewd V. "I won fair and square."

Alistair waved him off with a wrist flick. "Stephen beat Evan, so now Stephen chooses a name."

Georgie pointed at the mask overflowing with coins of all shapes and sizes. "The winner takes it all?" She could not care less about the money. When she won, she would pay Jimmy's debt.

"Yes. The loser must add another bob to the pot," Major Blythe said. "And no one has cheated. Not on my watch."

The earl and the duke both *harrumph*ed.

Stephen bent to pull a slip from the mask as Georgie mentally connected dots. If William Harrington was chosen and won…? Bloody hell.

"Astleyshire," Stephen said.

William loosened his cravat and flung it to the side. He undid a couple of buttons and rolled up his sleeves. There were those forearms again. Georgie swallowed.

Within seconds her twin and the duke saluted.

"*En garde*," called the major.

Neither man moved as they studied each other's mettle. As she predicted, William Harrington was the first to strike. He lunged with grace and agility—quite impressive for a frame sculpted from compact muscle.

However, Stephen was skilled at predicting his adversaries' next move. Even a fox could not outwit her twin, so neither would a pretentious duke.

Equally matched, the men danced around the ballroom as gracefully as skilled waltzers. They thrusted, parried, and riposted.

Georgie's fists clenched and her shoulders met her chin as she cheered for her brother.

The first point was awarded to Stephen, and she hopped about like an excited child. She stomped her foot the two times the duke scored.

Thankfully, the following point went to Stephen. Then she held her breath as swords clanged.

Perhaps Mrs. Teague, Millie, and every other female in the world was correct. William Harrington was a spectacular specimen. The way his thigh muscles expanded when he lunged. The corded veins in his strong hands. The thick, black hair that bounced with his movement. The rise and fall of his chest as he exerted himself. And his eyes. Good lord, those eyes.

William thrust low and his blade contacted Stephen's hip. Georgie groaned.

"This round goes to Astleyshire," Major Blythe called.

Stephen, always the good sport, let his sword fall to his side as he clasped the duke's hand. "Well done, my friend."

"I only won because you have been fighting for twenty minutes straight." Then the duke's eyes widened as his gaze slid to Georgie.

The boisterous men quieted, and Jimmy gasped.

"Georgie is the only one left."

William Harrington bowed. "The prize is yours, Lady Georgiana."

As her brothers let out various guttural sounds letting the duke know his words were unwise, Georgie flung herself into his space. Just like her sword was about to do, she stabbed him in the chest with her finger. "I will take the prize when I win!"

The man smirked. "I was the undisputed champion at Bedford and Cambridge."

Her finger jabbed with each syllable. "And I am the champion of Trent Castle."

****

They stood in the center of the makeshift *piste*, Georgie facing William as the man fluttered his thick lashes. If it were not for the blunted weapon, she would have sliced the damnable black fans off. She brought the blade to her face, then forward and down.

William languidly repeated the salute.

The man deserved to be run through, not treated like an honorable opponent. The Duke of Astleyshire was about to learn the most important lesson of his life—never underestimate the fighting skill of a woman.

Georgie channeled one of her heroines, the agile Signora Ermenegilda Cheli. Knees bent, right foot forward, weapon steady, her back arm raised, she prepared.

"*En garde!*"

Her sword extended as she lunged. Still smirking and straight-legged, William parried as if he were swatting a fly. Georgie growled. Back foot first, she slid until she was a safe distance away, then rethought her strategy. Resting the point of his blade against the ballroom floor, William crossed one foot over the other and again fluttered his lashes.

What the bloody hell?

"Don't be a fool, Astleyshire. She will run you through like a Turkish kebab," Stephen called.

"I warned him." Evan chuckled. "I wager she beats him three to one."

"Well, in that case…" The arse of a duke twirled

his sword in an all-out taunt.

How dare he mock her. She hit high outside, her foil aiming for his shoulder. He parried, then thrust low.

Testosterone filled the air as the men cheered.

Light on her feet, she pivoted, cut, and thrust. Her tutelage beneath the master Henry Charles Angelo, and training with three athletic brothers had prepared her for the most skilled of fighters.

Unfortunately, William Harrington had studied with the same instructor and had the added benefit of being permitted to spar whenever he chose. And his legs, almost twice as long as hers, allowed him to run about like a headless chicken. Therefore, minutes into their bout, she was sweating and breathless, and he was swinging the sword about while dancing a jig.

Anger would not do. She needed to keep her wits about her. Pulling out her best move, the *balestra*, she jumped, ran toward William, then lunged.

Since his blade pointed toward the ceiling, and his foolish leaping had him off balance, her tip made contact with his chest.

Major Blythe awarded the point to her as the men beat on the floors and walls with delight.

Since she wanted William to take her seriously, she felt vindicated the second her weapon jabbed him. And it did seem to get his head out of his arse since he bent his knees and took the ready position.

Much to Georgie's horror, William Harrington's intense gaze met hers and singeing heat shot through her.

His lips firm, he thrust. She parried. He countered, tapping her shoulder.

The crowd booed at William—probably because

they thought her the weaker opponent.

She exhaled and recovered.

Unfortunately, William earned the next point when his blade tapped her in the center of the chest.

"Boo, hiss," the audience chanted.

Georgie backed away, shook the man's appealing qualities from her mind, and got into the ready position.

The door banged against the wall.

"Georgiana!" her grandmother cried out.

The countess's body slammed against the pine floorboards a second before a sword jabbed Georgie's shoulder.

****

Georgie exhaled, then cut, and six inches of her locks tumbled onto the dressing table. The act was not pleasurable since her father had loved her long hair. But she had no choice because there was too much to tuck under her new Winkentattle wig.

She frowned at her reflection. It was probably still too long.

Without knocking, Millie barged into her bed chamber, slamming the door behind her. "Lady Georgiana, what are you doing?"

"Please calm yourself, Millie."

"But your beautiful hair. What would your father say?"

"'Tis not that short."

Georgie sighed and put down her embroidery shears. A few inches past her shoulders would have to do.

Millie watched with wide eyes as Georgie chopped a strand into tiny pieces. Then, dipping her fingers into a bowl of pitch Jimmy had collected for her, she coated her cheeks and stuck the tiny hairs into the tacky substance. She took her time molding two sideburns. Tilting her head from side to side, she studied her creation. Unfortunately, she looked like a woman who had glued hair to the side of her face.

Millie turned Georgie to the side and studied her. "I think I can fix it." She pruned as she talked. "The countess is requesting your presence in the drawing room. She would like to discuss preparations for the ball. She has promised tea and honey cakes."

Georgie's mouth watered as she rolled her eyes.

"If you do not go to her, she will come looking for you. And she cannot see you like this."

"Fine. Tell her I will be down as soon as I am dressed."

Millie wrinkled her nose. "Dressed like a boy?"

"No. Like myself," Georgie said. "But first, I need to improve my Winkentattle disguise. You heard what Peter and Christopher said."

Millie placed the shears on the vanity and smiled. "Better." She angled Georgie so they could both look into the mirror.

The sideburns were almost believable.

Millie pinned the wig into place as Georgie placed a strand of hair above her lip and grinned.

The mustache was a fabulous idea. Later that evening, she would attach the hair to a small strip of lace and use hide glue to affix it to her skin.

"The wig is better than the cap, but I still think your cheeks are a bit soft and pink for a man," Millie said.

Georgie hastened to the fireplace and dunked her hand in the ash bucket. Back at the dressing table, she ran a finger over her cheeks.

"Goldcount piled his coins into three large piles and chortled manically," declared Georgie in her best Winkentattle voice.

"Oh, Georgie. You are getting so good at that. And you look like a man except for the dress. Once you put on your waistcoat and breeches, no one will be the wiser."

The compliment should have thrilled Georgie. So, why did it leave her feeling like she wanted to flee into the night?

"Please tell my grandmother I will be right down."

"Christopher said that the fake story went out with peddlers. They were hidden beneath bags of ribbons and have been widely distributed."

"Perfect," Georgie said.

"There may be hundreds of villagers, some from the surrounding counties, coming to see Winkentattle."

One minute Millie was a bundle of fizzled nerves, and the next, she was encouraging Georgie. Perhaps that was due to her attraction to Christopher and her desire to take care of Georgie. Whatever the reason, Georgie was grateful for a companion she could share almost everything with.

She was about to confide her misgivings when Millie curtsied and exited the room.

Georgie gathered the clippings and hid them in a shiny silver box that had once been her mother's. She cleaned her sticky skin with a pilfered glass of Alistair's gin and scrubbed the soot from her cheeks. After weaving her hair into a French braid, she pinned the tail to her nape.

No one would know that it was shorter. And if it

was discovered, hopefully, William would appreciate the new style.

She grunted at her reflection. Why did William Harrington consume so much of her energy? She did not even like the man. Well, she might have come to appreciate certain attributes. But overall, he was still a pompous arse, and she would have won their match had he not been a rat bastard.

She tromped out of her room and down the hall. Those cakes had better be delicious.

And there better be scones with sweet orange jam.

Chapter Thirteen

December 27th, 1816

Maria Seraphina placed the mincemeat pie in front of the golden door and rapped three times before sprinting off to hide behind a tree. The door opened and a flat-snouted nose appeared. It sniffed and snorted. Then the baron peeked his entire head out and his beady eyes searched.
From Tattle's Tales

William was an arse! The Dashed Duke. The King of Fools. And all because Lady Georgiana Eaton *might* like his eyes. Even though she crinkled her nose as if she were smelling shite when in his presence; according to Jimmy, she did not hate everything about him. Although by shamelessly flirting with her in front of her brothers, he had probably solidified her opinion that he was nothing but a blimey bugger.

Not only was the lady beautiful and fascinating, she was also a worthy opponent in sport. And damn, that was intoxicating!

The spoils of the game scattered over his counterpane, reminding him of his ungentlemanly conduct the day before. Pushing the coins into a pile, he dropped onto the edge of his bed and rubbed his forehead. His thumping brain threatened to burst through his skull.

On his walk home with the young lad, things had changed for William, and he was not sure he could keep the promises made to the prince.

Awareness had crashed into him, knocking the breath from his lungs. The circumstances leading to the loss of Jimmy's arm were obvious to anyone with half a brain, and no child should ever be exploited so that some prick of a factory owner could become wealthier. The tables had turned, and despite his affection for his cousin, he would bring down the baron.

And, bedding a woman to win a bet, topped his growing list of deplorable qualities.

Not wanting to look at his ill-gotten gains one second longer, he emptied his small velvet travel sack and replaced his hairbrushes with the coins.

He found Georgiana in the drawing room, curled up on the settee. Her purple dress contrasted with her fair coloring in a most appealing way, and her shoes sat on the floor in front of her. She held a piece of paper and chewed on the end of a pencil. Her eyes widened, then she scribbled. What he would not give to know what she wrote.

Damn, she was beautiful. Her red hair was shorter than he had thought, but it was deliciously disheveled, making her look like she had recently been ravaged. Her emerald eyes, intensely studying her writing, epitomized intelligence. The freckles dotting her nose and creamy skin were kissable. And, oh, that plump bosom and healthy figure that a man could worship and sink into. Fuck, his balls ached.

He stepped into the room and cleared his throat.

She looked up from her writing and her cheeks

flushed.

He strolled across the room and held out the peace offering. "I think this is yours."

She frowned at the bag dangling from his fingers. "What is it?"

"The purse from our bout," he said.

She glowered.

"I owe you an apology."

"Oh?"

"Could I join you?" He inclined his chin toward the end of the settee her legs occupied.

She sighed and hesitated before dropping her feet to the floor and sliding them into her slippers.

He had not even arranged his coattails when she leaned into his space. "Do not underestimate an opponent because they were born into this world female."

He held up a palm. "I would never—"

"Why are you offering me a prize I have not yet won?"

"I was a fool. After watching you fight—"

She stood. "You are a fool, William Harrington. Your final point was earned in a most dishonorable way. You ran about the *piste* like a clown making a joke of our bout. In a fair fight, I would stab you through your heartless chest."

Heartless? And, never before had his attempts at flirting been called clownish. The woman had him off-kilter.

She leaned over him, forcing him to push his back against the cushion if he wanted to look into her eyes instead of gawking at the soft swell of her bosom.

Her expression contained hellfire. "I shall show

you what I am truly capable of."

His heart sped up.

She backed up and stomped to the door. Before exiting the room, she spun to face him. "Are you coming?"

"*Umm.* Yes." He would follow this lovely enigma to the ends of the earth just as soon as he talked down his growing cock.

****

Lady Georgiana wore men's clothes. By God— men's breeches and boots! However, there was nothing masculine about her feminine curves that peeked out from the woman's bodice.

He had stood outside her chamber, shuffling his feet while she changed, praying that no one asked him what he was doing. He had no idea what he was doing. Only that she had told him to wait there, so he had.

Now, she squatted and then bounded into the air five times, her heels coming so high off the ground they hit her buttocks. Thereupon, she hopped from one foot to the other for a good three minutes. Finally, her arms swung in large circles at least eight times each.

"Now I am ready," she said while retrieving a sword from the pile of weapons that still lay on the ballroom floor. "My grandmother is resting, so there will be no swooning today."

Good thing since the poor countess would surely break a hip if she kept landing on the hardwood.

Georgiana lifted her sword into the ready position.

William followed her lead. "Three taps?" he asked.

Biting her lip, she hesitated before saying, "To the death." Her green eyes glimmered, a malapert grin replaced her thoughtful look, and then she lunged.

Disarmed by her comment and impish smile, he was not prepared, so her sword tapped his chest. He attempted to sound affronted despite his absolute delight at her mischievous side.

"My lady, now who is behaving in an unchivalrous manner?"

"Fine, that did not count. However, there is no official to start us," she said, her expression wicked.

Palm up, he rolled his hand while performing his most elegant bow. "Be my guest."

Their gazes locked and she whispered, "*En garde*." Her bold movements in no way matched her soft voice. Performing a *fleche*, she ran toward him and feinted that she meant to hit low. As he parried, she struck high inside.

"One to zero." She backed up and got into the ready position.

William needed to ignore his thrumming cock and give this woman the fight she deserved.

This time when she advanced, his sword met hers. Although he was stronger and quite agile for his size, she moved with the deftness of a feline. She also predicted his every move, making them equally matched.

On the offensive, she thrust. His sword caught and moved with hers. After a particularly high outside hit, he used his strength to his advantage, caught her sword with his, pushed it in a circle, and down and away from him.

"Bloody hell," she grumbled as her booted foot slid on the slippery floor. As she steadied herself, he tapped her shoulder.

"Two, one," he said with a grin.

She stepped back, and her knees bent so much that she looked more like a ninja than a fencer.

"*En garde,*" she growled.

The clang of metal hitting metal provided an exhilarating musicality. She pushed him out of the *piste* and across the room with progressive actions. Spinning, her sword collided with his. She turned again and parried.

A whirling dervish met his counter-attack. Step, spin, parry, step, spin, parry. She was a blur of hair and silver blade.

Step, spin, kick! Her heel walloped his stomach. His sword flew from his hand, and he stumbled backward, smashing into the wall.

She was in front of him instantly. The tip of her blade pressed into his neck, her opposite forearm held him in place, and her breathy words blew across his cheek. "William Harrington, I will not be courted by you."

Bright eyes. Flushed cheeks. Labored breaths. A woman exerting herself in sport had a lot in common with one who was just about to scream her pleasure.

"I have not asked to court you." *Yet.*

Her blunted tip dug into his flesh. "When I win, you will return to Hockley Castle, and this nonsense will end."

Her aggressive tactics had the opposite effect, making him want to stay longer. "And when I win…"

He wrapped an arm around her waist, pulled her against him, and inhaled. Lavender and roses, mingled with sweating woman. Delicious.

Surely a kiss was not the same as bedding a woman to win a wager.

"I want a kiss," he whispered.

Was that a whimper that followed the hitch in her breath?

She pulled from his grasp, stepped back, and blinked. "Two, two." She swooped to the ground, retrieved his sword, and tossed it.

He grabbed the hilt as easily as catching a firefly on a summer eve, but before he could prepare, she lunged.

No rules. Fine by him. He ducked and came out on the other side of her.

She didn't miss a beat. Again, she cut high. Their swords and hands locked above their heads, their gazes bore into each other's souls, and their lips were so close, all he had to do was lean forward a few inches. His pressure matched her pressure until she shoved him and stepped away.

He needed to be patient because the little hellcat would surely kick again. But how in the blazes was he supposed to concentrate with her heaving bosom and heavy panting?

At last, she shifted her weight into her back foot as her front leg lifted.

He grabbed her extended calf and tugged, pulling her off balance. As they tumbled, he held his sword away from her and flipped their positions so she landed on top of him.

Thunk. He absorbed the shock as the ballroom floor reverberated. He tapped his blade into her shoulder. "Three, two," he said as he slid his sword to the side.

Although her blade dug into him, he was fairly certain the expression on her face was elation. Obviously, the woman enjoyed a good fight. And he had given her one.

With her blunted sword still at his throat, he bravely wrapped an arm around her waist. "I think you owe me my prize kiss, my lady."

He expected her to punch him in the nose and then leap off him. Instead, she lay there, her body pressing against his.

He batted his lashes.

A gasp escaped from those kissable lips.

He placed his mouth next to her delicate pink earlobe. "One little kiss." Removing the sword from her loose grip, he pushed it to the side. Then his hand threaded through her luscious hair so that he could guide her mouth to his.

At first tentative, her soft lips parted. Since her warm body melted into his, he deepened the kiss as she caressed his cheek.

While in his arms, the fiery fighter had become an innocent angel who tasted of strawberries and cream.

A moment later, she hopped off his aching body and fled from the room.

He brought a hand to his forehead and moaned. Damn his cock to hell. Since it had stabbed her through layers of fabric, it had probably scared her off.

Seconds later, he chuckled. What in the hell was his mission? Something about the Prince Regent, Handershane, and Evan Eaton. Whatever the hell it was, he had more important tasks at hand.

Like courting Lady Georgiana Eaton.

Chapter Fourteen

December 28th, 1816

"Mmm." Goldcount's balls tightened in anticipation as the fragrant spices swirled around him. At last, he spied the pie. He dropped to his knees, closed his eyes, and inhaled. Unable to take it a second longer, he shoved his snout into the dish.
From Tattle's Tales

It was late afternoon when Georgie cuddled next to her twin and rested her head on his shoulder. The flames from the Yule log still burned hot, enveloping her in holiday warmth. She scooted closer to Stephen, and he kissed her on the top of her head. Closing her eyes, she willed the moment to last forever.

"Georgie." Stephen moved his shoulder, jostling her. "My arm is falling asleep."

"*Humph,*" she murmured, ignoring him and shoving her head back where it had previously rested.

He bombarded her with a dozen finger flicks that were so annoying that she had to sit up.

"Your arm obviously has enough blood pumping into it to do this." She flicked him back and rolled onto her back, placing her head in his lap. "Napoleon was defeated. Why must you go to London?"

The index finger and thumb that had been

tormenting her pushed the corners of her mouth into a smile.

She swatted his hand away. "Do you not want to come home?"

"Well, yes. I suppose." Stephen stared into the fire with an indecipherable expression.

"But?"

"Alistair is running the estate, so there is little for me to do here. I will be continuing my military appointment in London."

Georgie's protests puffed up her cheeks. London was closer than France, but it was not Trent Castle.

"Eventually I want to marry and have a family. This war has taught me what is precious. And 'tis what Mother and Father would have wanted." Stephen pushed up on her jaw, the same way he did when they were little, and he wanted to stop her from pouting. "Georgie, we cannot stay children forever. We have to embrace change and growth."

"I plan to stay here with Alistair. I will never marry. This is my home." She sighed because Stephen was correct. She was behaving like a child instead of a woman of one-and-twenty.

He peered down at her, forcing her to look into his eyes. "Trent Castle will always be a part of you. But keep in mind, Alistair will not marry before you."

"Stop talking in riddles. What does that mean?"

Stephen chuckled. "You, my dear sister, can fend for yourself. So, the three of us are in no way trying to find a man to take care of you." He tapped her nose. "However, 'tis Alistair's responsibility to make sure you have a family of your own to love. You know Mother and Father loved each other. And although

Grandmother was forced into an arranged marriage, she came to love Grandfather. I think she feels the same will happen for you."

How could she articulate her feelings?

"Benjamin Calhoun is a good person. He is only a fourth son, but I know you don't care about money or land, and his family is quite respected. He is not the type of man who would try to mold you into something you are not. He will be a good husband and father. However…" Stephen's forehead wrinkled.

"But I do not love Benjamin."

"I know. And I am not sure you would be happy with a soldier."

Georgie nodded. "He will make another woman a brave husband."

"You need a companion. Someone to match wits with," Stephen said.

Georgie was tired of saying it, but she would repeat it one more time. "I do not need a husband. I need a puppy."

"And Astleyshire?" Stephen asked.

"A puppy would do him good, too. Knock some of that arrogance out of him."

"I meant, could you love the duke?"

"I hate William Harrington," she spat.

Stephen chuckled. "You could have fooled me."

She sat up so that she could better glare at her brother. "What do you mean by that?"

"I see the way you look at him. And he is a match for your fire."

"I do not look at him." Please, God. Don't strike her down for lying. "He is a womanizing prig. I have no idea why, but he is only here to torment me and get back at Evan over some woman." Georgie gagged. "An older woman, no less."

"I think it has more to do with a card game gone bad. And older women are often very attractive to younger men. They make wonderful companions." Stephen ruffled her hair as if she were a clueless child. "And Astleyshire is quite infatuated with you."

Her indignantly snapped chin shot pain down her arm. "Why would you say that? He made an absolute fool of himself running about the ballroom, not taking me seriously. I would hardly call that infatuation."

Kissing her until her body trembled might be infatuation. Although, more than likely, that was his legendary roguish shenanigans.

"Most men have never fenced with a woman and would have refused the bout with you. He did not."

He, in fact, had come back the next day and given her a hell of a fight.

"Forgive my sex, but sometimes when we want to know a woman better, we behave like damn fools," Stephen said.

"But he and Evan despise each other. And he is in league with Handershane."

"As for his friendship with Handershane, I do not buy it. His jaw and fist clench every time the baron speaks to him. And who do you love the most in the entire world?" Stephen asked.

"You, Alistair, and Evan." She balked. "And Grandmother." She held up a hand to tick off, "Jimmy, Millie, Cook, Mrs. T—"

"Do you not see the similarities?"

Georgie rested her head on the back of the settee and exhaled. "What similarities?"

"William Harrington takes his responsibilities as seriously as Alistair takes his?"

Was that true?

"And Evan and Astleyshire detest each other because they are so much alike."

"*Hmm?*" By God, they were.

"So, the man you are avoiding has things in common with two men you love."

Stephen had always been insightful.

"Is William also like you?" Georgie asked.

Stephen shrugged. "That is hard to say. I do not quite know how others perceive me."

"Chivalrous, brave, heroic, thoughtful." None of those qualities defined the Duke of Astleyshire.

Stephen's eyes twinkled. "I hope I am all of those things."

She snuggled up against him again. "I wish you did not have to leave tonight and could stay for the Twelfth Night Ball. The countess needs someone to keep her from going overboard." Although, no matter how much she wished for it, if he stayed, he might be in danger due to Winkentattle's words.

"That responsibility falls on you, sister. But remember, Louisa Eaton is a grandmother and mother with a beating heart beneath all of that stoic etiquette. She simply wants us to marry and give her great-grandchildren to fawn over."

This time, Stephen sprawled on his back and rested his head in Georgie's lap. "Tell me a story. One with a knight and a dragon. Then, I will kick your arse. First one to get ten taps wins the other's mincemeat pie."

"I will take that wager," Georgie said.

Mincemeat pies were almost as good as honey cakes.

And winning was better than them both.

Chapter Fifteen

December 28, 1816

*While Goldcount snuffled mincemeat, Jackson
Valiant tiptoed up behind him and clobbered him on the
back of the head. Goldcount lay motionless, his face in
a pie and his large arse splayed for everyone to kick.*
From Tattle's Tales

The countess and her grandsons were quite
loquacious, devouring platters and tureens of food. All
in all, the Eaton family, with their zest for everything—
food, sport, laughter, and kinship were endearing
themselves to William. Still, Evan needed to be brought
down a few pegs, and Lady Georgiana needed to smile
more when in William's presence.

Although she sat diagonally from him, she refused
to meet his gaze, and she spent most of the dinner
silently smashing baked parsnips flat against her plate.
It was most disconcerting since she had eaten as much
as two large men for most of his visit.

The multiple conversations surrounding him came
to a halt when the countess addressed her middle
grandson.

"I do not know why you must part tonight. Why
not stay and leave in the light of day?"

"We must reunite with the 2nd Life Guards this

evening. They were dispatched a week before us to halt uprisings farther south. We will travel back to London together," Stephen said.

"I do not understand," Lady Georgiana said. "How many battalions were employed to stop uprisings? Are they expected all over the country?"

"Hopefully not," Stephen said. "I am of the opinion that it is an overreaction. I don't see any evidence of uprisings. I read the most recent *Tattle's Tales*. It was mostly about charity during the holiday season. It portrayed the royal family and the aristocracy favorably. Really, quite funny. Although the factory owner bloke was ridiculous." Stephen slapped the table and chuckled. "A goat chasing him through town in his night shift."

Lady Georgiana's peachy complexion turned an odd shade of off-white. "I still do not understand. Why send so many soldiers over such a wide area?"

"Lady Georgiana, Winkentattle is quite the troublemaker," William said as he sent Evan a death glance. "Peddlers are delivering these stories from Leeds to Birmingham." William checked himself. He no longer cared about outing Evan or spying. He was only there for kisses.

"The *ton* has panicked," said Stephen. "They expect Winkentattle to explain the Corn Tax in his stories and support reforms in Parliament next."

For a second, Georgiana's eyes lit up. "The Corn Tax," she murmured under her breath.

"Again, it seems to be an overreaction," Stephen said.

"Enough about this unpleasant topic," said the countess. "Why are Major Blythe and the second lieutenant not joining us for dinner? They should eat well before their travel."

William did not miss Calhoun in the least. He was done watching the young soldier blush and drool all over the redhead.

Georgiana stopped playing with her food to gaze at her twin. Her sad expression tore at William's heart.

"Grandmother, do stop fretting," Stephen said. "They are dining with our men and Cook is making sure they are well-fed. Warm soup, bread, cheese, eggs, and mincemeat pies." Stephen frowned at his pie and slid it to his sister. "Here."

At last. That spectacular smile.

"Let us share," she said to Stephen.

"I would be most delighted."

The twins dug into the pie at the same time. Chortles ripped from them as they tried to outdo each other by taking the bigger bite.

The countess brought a hand to her chest, and her face contorted with disgust. "My heavens! Your mother would never have allowed such behavior at the table. And Stephen you are a captain."

Stephen winced and set down his utensil. Georgiana shoveled in two more bites before putting down her fork and sighing.

The countess folded her hands in front of her. "The invitations for the Twelfth Night Ball went out. The ballroom will be turned into a delightful apple orchard. Oh, Stephen, I wish you could stay and see the trees the florist created. A thousand candles will light the room. There will be carved benches all about. Even the food is themed. Cider with cinnamon. Apple tarts. Pork with baked apples. And the mincemeat pies will be adorned with an apple cutout."

"You have outdone yourself, Grandmother," Alistair said.

The countess preened. "I have asked everyone to dress in red, green, white, and gold."

Lady Georgiana looked divine in emerald. No, red. The lady in red. Wait, gold. Dear God. She should definitely wear gold.

"Alistair, I hope you will find time to dance with Arabella Beaumont," the countess said.

Evan and Stephen chuckled as Georgiana rolled her eyes. Alistair gulped.

The lady was undaunted by her less-than-enthusiastic grandchildren. "I have invited Lord and Lady Doolittle. Maybe Miss Bethany Doolittle would be to your liking, Evan."

Evan cringed. "Bethany wears feathers so large she can barely hold her head up."

"Mayhap Lady Hemmingsworth would be more to his liking." Lady Georgiana's smile resembled a satisfied smirk.

"Your Grace, I do hope that you can find room on your dance card for our Georgiana," the countess said.

"I do not dance," the redhead growled.

Of course not.

"What a shame. A woman with your athletic skill would make a glorious dance partner." William scrutinized her expression. "Mayhap Arabella Beaumount and Bethany Doolittle will have openings on their dance cards for me."

Was that pouting lip jealousy? He could work with jealousy.

"And the Widow Hemmingsworth and I are old

friends." William smiled at Georgiana then smirked at Evan. "She always saves a dance for me."

Evan's eyes darkened.

Stephen stood. "I am afraid I must be on my way."

"No," Lady Georgiana said, tears filling her green eyes.

She clung to him, breaking William's heart. Evan eventually pried her fingers from their brother and held Georgie in his arms as Stephen took his leave.

Georgie wiped the tears from her eyes. "I shall go to the library to read." Her shoulders slumped as she left the room.

"Duke, how about a game of cards?" Evan asked.

"Splendid," Alistair said.

"I shall spend time with Georgiana this evening. Maybe planning the ball will cheer her up," said the countess as she stood. "Excuse me, gentlemen. Enjoy your cards."

William suspected that conversations about the ball would not bring even a half a second of joy to the redhead. And he preferred to spend the evening in the library fluttering his lashes at her.

However, he resigned himself to an evening with the men.

He followed the brothers to Alistair's study. Cards were dealt. Cheroots were lit. Port was poured.

Maybe Georgiana Eaton might enjoy reading him one of those books she loved so much. He could rest his head on her lap and look up at her as she narrated exciting tales.

His body filled with some foreign sensation. Warm, tingly, and peaceful.

"Hey, Duke," Evan said. "'Tis your turn."

Shaking off daydreams to concentrate on cards was one hell of a difficult task.

Chapter Sixteen

December 29th, 1816

Goldcount used the sleeve of his tunic to wipe away the pie. Then he waved his hands about as if swatting flies. "I know this was the two of you, Jackson Valiant and Maria Seraphina. And when I find you, I will rip out your hearts and feed them to the village swine."
From Tattle's Tales

Millie's blue cloak and full skirts swirled around her as she and Georgie dashed across the lawn to the shadowy treeline, where Christopher and Peter, wearing dark clothes and sitting atop black horses, waited. Since Georgie wore breeches, it was easy for Peter to grasp her hand and pull her onto the saddle behind him.

Christopher dropped to the ground, locked his hands together forming a step, and hoisted Millie into the saddle before climbing up to join her.

"Your plan worked, Lady Georgiana," Christopher said. "The Boxing Day edition had enough humor and joy to placate readers. The soldiers are gone. Our men are ready to converge on the factory and Handershane's house, and a crowd has already gathered in the village."

Peter's evil laugh sent a chill up Georgie's spine. "Gangs of joyous wassailers overtaking the streets are keeping anyone from being the wiser."

"Handershane's wife and children are still in London? They will not be injured in any way, correct?" Georgie asked.

"Aye," Christopher said. "Although he has no scruples about hurting others' wives and children."

"Christopher," Millie said, her tone reproving. She placed a hand on his forearm.

A horse whinnied. Then, all was quiet as the cold night absorbed sound. Christopher clucked his tongue as he aimed his mare toward the village. Footsteps crunched piercing the stillness.

"Who goes there?" Peter pulled a pistol from his waistband.

"Wait." Georgie held up a hand. The other rested on the handle of the sword hanging at her side.

"'Tis me, Lady Georgie," said a child.

"Do not shoot."

Georgie's eyes played tricks in the darkness, distorting every shadow into the enemy. She rubbed them before double-checking to see who stood in front of her. A pointless endeavor since she did not need eyesight. Only one child would follow her in the dark.

"Jimmy, what are you doing here?"

"I wanted to make sure you and Millie were safe," Jimmy said.

"My boy, head back to the castle," Christopher said.

Sadness filled the normally optimistic boy's voice. "I can still help with one arm."

"Of course, you can," Georgie said. "You can do anything. But I gave you the most important job. You must keep Alistair and Evan from leaving the castle."

It was not just imperative, it would keep Jimmy out

of harm's way, allowing Georgie to focus on her task.

"Please make haste."

"Yes, my lady." Jimmy bowed before scurrying in the direction he had come from.

"Please be careful," Millie called after him.

Georgie exhaled affection and breathed in anxiety. She closed her eyes and let go of everything before filling her lungs with her cause. Really, she had no other choice because her ability to tell a grand story was a gift she needed to use to incite change. First came better working conditions. After that, social justice for all.

Moments later, she matched her breaths to the clomp of the horses' hooves.

They were halfway to the village when Georgie palmed her forehead. Why had she not asked Jimmy to also keep the nosey duke from leaving the castle?

****

Rush lanterns, candlewicks, and a few gas streetlights lit up the scene like a million fireflies on a summer eve. Paperboys stood on the outskirts handing out the same colorful edition of *Tattle's Tales* that she was about to read. Songs and chatter echoed back and forth between the buildings. So many men and women roamed the square that Georgie's party struggled to navigate the crowd. To her surprise, much of her audience had partaken of too much ale, and red-nosed children ran amok.

If it were not for the men armed with everything from bayonets to bludgeons escorting them through the throng to a slipshod stage, one would think it was a holiday festivity. Once they reached the platform, Georgie tested her foot on a thin step and the wood sagged. Meanwhile, flurries fell from the sky, landing on her shoulders and wig. She licked the flakes from her lips and breathed.

"Are you ready, Winkentattle?" Christopher asked.

If the heavy feeling in the pit of her gut was terror, then Georgie had never felt anything even close to fear before. She removed her paper from the satchel at her waist and pulled her shoulders back. "Yes."

Someone handed her a rush lantern. Georgie stood in the center of the flimsy stage. She held the lantern in one hand and her chapbook in the other. Legs that normally held her as steady as a mighty oak trembled, reminding her of how she felt about William Harrington.

What was wrong with her? She had avoided the man for the past two days so His Royal Arsewipe should be the furthest thing from her mind. She was not Lady Georgiana, the silly woman who grew weak in the knees around a muscled aristocrat. She was Winkentattle, the fearless man with the quick wit and magic pen, who had become the voice of the working class.

Yes. That was exactly who she was. Pulling her alter ego into every pore of her being, her stance widened. She cleared her throat and channeled the deep voice residing in her belly. Her arm lifted and she waved.

The crowd hushed as hundreds of expectant eyes stared up at her.

"Good evening, everyone. Let me tell you the tale about the time Jackson Valiant and Maria Seraphina thwarted Baron Goldcount using their wits, a club, and a mincemeat pie."

Cheers ripped through the night, and the energy of at least five hundred suppressed villagers flooded Georgie, coming out in her battle cry that reached the heavens.

Chapter Seventeen

December 29th, 1816

Goldcount's limbs flailed about as he sputtered obscenities. A misplaced foot on a particularly slippery raisin halted his theatrics, and he landed on his arse with a thud.
From Tattle's Tales

The audience hung on every one of Winkentattle's words. As his voice rose, they stood on tiptoe, when he imitated a female, hands landed on hearts. When the buffoon Goldcount spoke, they jeered.

Since it was quite entertaining, William did his best to concentrate on the story. However, his mind whirled because he had been mistaken. The man on stage was not Evan Eaton. The man on stage wasn't even a man. He was a boy of not much more than seven-and-ten. Sure, something about him resembled Evan. No, wait. He resembled a younger, slighter Stephen. However, the captain's regiment was days away.

"Maria Seraphina pummeled Goldcount in the nose. 'How dare you, you heartless swine!' The indignant baron meant to step back, but he slipped in cow shite, landing on his arse," Winkentattle read.

The audience chortled.

A tiny person at the edge of the crowd caught

William's attention. The child could not have been more than two-and-ten, and the sleeve of his coat folded over a handless wrist.

William groaned. Standing amongst this rowdy crowd who had imbibed too much cider and ale was no place for the young lad. Now he would have to keep one eye on Winkentattle and the other on Jimmy. Although any attention he gave Winkentattle was out of curiosity because he was done spying.

Perhaps someone else despised Evan as much as he and had started the rumor leading to the suspensions.

Whatever? Curse spying. To hell with Handershane.

Not all was lost. He was enjoying his time at Trent Castle. He had won every game of cards and every fencing match and was hell-bent on courting Georgiana Eaton. After all, he did love a challenge.

As soon as he returned to the castle, he would pour himself a drink, warm himself by the fire, then seek out the lady. She may be avoiding him since the kiss. But she could not avoid him forever.

The woman could act like she wasn't interested in him, but her sideways glances at dinner said otherwise, as did her body when it melted beneath him during that kiss. Besides, she liked his eyes. He chuckled.

"A sniveling Goldcount knelt in front of Jackson Valiant. Tears coated his cheeks, and he used the sleeve of his fine linen to wipe the snot from his nose."

A pretty woman jumped as she clapped. The hood of her cloak fluttered downward, landing on her shoulders and her blonde curls bounced about in the breeze.

Bloody hell! Lady Georgiana's maid stood with her

back pressed against a large man.

William pushed to the outskirts of the crowd, searching for a spot where he could better take in the scene. His attention darted between the man on stage, Lady Georgiana's maid, and Jimmy.

A thumping reverberated from far off. It did not appear that anyone else took notice. Even the beasts perched at the edges of the crowd had abandoned the stances of sentries to listen to the story. William cocked his ear toward the forest. The earth vibrated.

"Bloody hell!" William shoved his way through the crowd. "Jimmy!"

The army of Redcoats and sleek horses descended on the village in seconds. As large as William was, panicked people knocked him about as if he weighed mere ounces. Diminutive Jimmy would be crushed.

The child disappeared behind a wall of waving arms.

The man beside William held up a bludgeon and bellowed, "To the factory!"

"To the factory! To the factory!" the crowd chanted. Did they not understand that the Frame-Breaking Act was punishable by death? The damn fools were all going to die.

"Jimmy!" William yelled. "Jimmy!"

The boy's head bobbed between a woman wielding a tree limb and a man screeching filth. "Your Grace," Jimmy called, reaching out a hand.

However, soldiers had dismounted and joined the melee, and in the unruly sea of bodies, the boy was knocked farther from William's grasp.

An elbow caught William in the chin. At that moment, everyone keeping him from the boy became his enemy. His fingers clenched and his fist struck skin. Once, twice, three times. His fourth punch landed on a soldier's jaw.

At last, he reached the lad. "What in the blazes are you doing here?" William yelled over the uproar.

"I followed you."

William clutched Jimmy's coat so that they would not be separated. "Come on!"

A soldier reaching for the boy received an uppercut from William's free hand. He shook out his clenched fingers before tugging on Jimmy.

"No!" Jimmy cried. "Millie!"

William exhaled as he skimmed the tumult. Millie's blonde curls made her easy to spot and the large man she was with escorted her into the woods.

"She is safe." William knocked a burly villager in a black cap backward, then pilfered the man's knife. "Come on. *Now*."

"But… Lady Georgie!"

William stopped shoving bodies and his legs grew roots where he stood. "Lady Georgiana is here?"

"We have to help her." Jimmy dragged William toward the stage where villagers and soldiers warred. A rouge lantern rolled across the wood, then flames ate a corner of the platform.

Redcoats surrounded Winkentattle. He held a sword and it appeared he was about to thrust. Instead, he kicked with so much force that two soldiers careened into one another and toppled to the ground. Winkentattle spun, thrust, and his sword sliced his third opponent.

Impressive! Winkentattle, the one-man army.

Jimmy led William up the steps onto the burning

platform. "Help her."

"Where in the blazes is she?"

Jimmy freed himself from William's grasp and planted himself between Winkentattle and a blood-covered soldier. The boy squared his shoulders and growled.

Winkentattle's chest heaved as his sword lifted. Predatory did not begin to describe the man's intimidating stance.

Throwing an elbow into whoever lurked behind him, William yelled, "Jimmy, for deuce's sake, where is she?"

William and Winkentattle made eye contact for the first time.

William knew those eyes. He knew that stance. He knew that anger.

The injured Redcoat who stood between William and Georgiana Eaton moved quickly, aiming a pistol at Jimmy's head.

William had no desire to kill a soldier doing his duty, especially an injured one who held his weapon between trembling fingers. However, the young boy had followed him and was his responsibility. And he would give his life before he allowed anything to happen to the lady.

With a split-second, instinctual decision, he whipped his small weapon at the man's outstretched arm. Georgiana leaped and kicked. Her toe met the man's chin. He plummeted off the stage as the pistol flew, landing at William's feet.

William swooped down to pick it up just as a shot rang out. When he stood, three soldiers pointed guns at Georgiana as flames crackled and popped engulfing the scene.

She dropped her sword to the ground and her gaze slid to Jimmy.

William understood that wordless plea. While all eyes were on Winkentattle's arrest, he navigated the smoke, swung Jimmy over his shoulder, and took off into the woods.

Chapter Eighteen

December 29th, 1816

While the baron snored and dreamed of gold coins growing from trees, Jackson and Maria tiptoed into his chamber.
From Tattle's Tales

Although Georgie rarely cried, tears stung her eyes. Mostly because she was trying not to choke on the chapbook that a glowering sergeant had wadded up and shoved into her mouth. Ironically, it was a strip of lace tied around her head that kept her from spitting out her own words. Moreover, the burlap sack encasing her from head to waist was most disorienting.

She worked her cheeks and tongue, attempting to push the paper as far from her esophagus as possible. As she tilted her head from side to side, the lace loosened. Nothing budged. She tested the bindings around her wrists. With each tug, they grew tighter. The same was true of the ropes digging into her ankles.

The front wheels of the wagon hit something and the warm bodies around her were jostled. Perhaps thirty men and women sat squished together. It was hard to tell since no one spoke. The stench from fear and sweaty bodies mingled together and filtered through the sack. Adding insult to injury, the entire fiasco was

Georgie's fault.

Without her sight, the pictures in her mind became more vivid. The blood on the tip of her sword. Millie's horrified, wide-eyed expression. The pistol aimed at a child's head. And the man who had saved Jimmy.

Even though the boy was prepared to stop William from tearing Winkentattle limb from limb, the duke had still come to Jimmy's rescue. This somehow made William's action even more heroic.

Harrington may have been an arrogant fool, but every fiber of her being told her that Jimmy had been safely returned to Trent Castle. But was William responsible for the soldiers being there? And where was Stephen? She prayed he had not been injured.

Not only did the blindfold heighten Georgie's imagery, but her hearing was also on high alert.

Horsehooves trotted toward them, and the wagon halted. Georgie tilted her head to make sense of muffled words, catching, "…on the way to Newgate."

Newgate? Dear Lord! Diseases. Filth. Torture. And at the rate they were traveling, it would take them days on that freezing, uncomfortable wagon. How had everything gone so wrong?

"Do you have Winkentattle among your prisoners?"

Georgie would know that deep baritone anywhere.

"Yes, Your Grace."

"I have been charged with escorting Winkentattle to the prince," William Harrington said.

Georgie's shoulders tensed.

"We have not received word of that."

"I have my missive right here," William said.

The longer the silence lasted, the faster Georgie's

heart beat.

Finally, someone spoke. "Captain, 'tis the royal seal. The letter says the Duke of Astleyshire is tasked with escorting Winkentattle."

What in tarnation? She knew the man was up to no good. And she had allowed him to kiss her. At least the captain's muffled response was not her twin's voice.

"Yes. I am to personally deliver the traitor to the prince," William said.

"My Grace, the letter does not say that."

"Obviously, 'tis what it means. Are you arguing with a duke?"

"No, Your Grace."

"I can travel three times as fast with the prisoner alone. The prince plans to make an example of him for all to see. Swish!" William chuckled.

William was probably slicing the edge of his hand across his neck and enjoying an image of her head popping from her body.

She fought her binds with everything she had. As soon as she broke free, she would cut out the duke's heart. Except, he did not have a heart. So, she would slice him into bite-sized pieces and feed him to a thousand rats.

At least two sets of hands grabbed her and dragged her off the wagon.

"Help me get him onto my horse," William said.

A foot landed square in her gut and she tumbled to the ground. Something slammed into her back.

"Do not kill the fellow yet. Let His Royal Highness have that pleasure," William said.

After being tossed about like a rag doll, she ended up draped over a horse, her head dangling on one side, her feet on the other; her bound hands and arse protruding toward the sky.

"Godspeed," someone yelled.

"Thank you," William said to her captors. His lips brushed her ear. "Do not say a word."

No problem since her larynx contained lace and inked paper.

William mounted the horse with his pelvis pressed against her side. He slapped her on the buttocks. She wriggled and he chuckled. Thereupon, he bellowed for all to hear, "Be still, Winkentattle."

She grunted. Not that it was audible.

William clicked his tongue, and they were off.

Her head bounced, hitting the horse's flank so often that she became nauseous. However, it may have been worth it since the friction loosened the lace enough that she spit out the paper and no longer feared choking to death. She lost all concepts of time and direction, and every inch of her body ached.

Still, she schemed. William had no idea who she was, and she would keep her disguise in place. Eventually, he would sleep.

Then Winkentattle would free himself and strangle the dashing duke with the same ropes that bound her hands.

Chapter Nineteen

December 29th, 1816

Baron Goldcount searched high and low for his cravats. They were nowhere to be found.
From Tattle's Tales

What in the hell was he thinking? After returning Jimmy to Trent Castle, he had falsified a document using his family's seal. It was not even a good forgery. So, when the Crown discovered that he had helped a traitor escape, he would join the rioters at Newgate.

The things this woman did to him.

And now she was pressed against his frigging cock with her hindquarters jutting into the air—and he had patted that luscious *derrière*. A man responsible for most of the Mid Eastlands and he spanked injured ladies on their sweet arses. Would he ever grow out of his damn randiness?

If he died this very evening, he was going to hell. If he lived a hundred more years, he was going to hell. Bloody hell! He was going to hell. At least he would spend eternity warm.

Navigating trees in the moonlight proved a daunting task. He pulled his gelding into a clearing and rubbed his eyes. Hopefully, by now, they were far away from the caravan heading to London.

Georgiana moaned.

He slid off Lightning and worked at the bindings on her ankles. "Do not kick me."

Although Georgiana whimpered, she did not move. He attempted to work faster, but his numb fingers struggled with the knots. Once her legs were free, he grasped her calves and tugged her upper body onto the top of the horse. Cradling her waist, he set her down gently. Her feet touched the ground, and her body swayed as she balanced. She stood still for a moment before lashing out.

Caught off guard, he stumbled backward. Unlike her kicks a couple of days ago, this one was not strong enough to do any damage. The woman really was in poor shape.

"I do not need my hands or eyes. Come near me, and I will kick you all the way to hell," said a deep voice.

William did a double take. Was she still playing at being the male Winkentattle? And did she think he was the enemy? His spunky Georgiana—believing she could defeat him in her current condition? Oh, to have that passion between his sheets.

He chuckled.

She brought her left foot forward and crouched. "Do not try me." She growled. "Laugh one more time and I will make sure you never laugh again."

He stepped to the right, and she squared her shoulders to him. Perhaps she could track him in that hood.

"I cannot untie your hands if you plan to kill me," he said.

"Then do not untie me," the deep-voiced

Winkentattle said. "I told you I do not need hands."

She dashed toward him so quickly that he barely had time to prepare. He took a kick to the groin that dropped him to his knees.

"Fuck!" He panted out the pain with his groan. With her next strike, he caught her ankle, yanked her onto the ground, and pinned her beneath him. "I am trying to help you."

"I do not need your help."

She was so damn determined that he would indulge her fantasy. He placed his lips on the outline of her ear. "I beg to differ, *Mr.* Winkentattle. You were on your way to the gallows."

Christ, she was prickly.

"And you think carrying me off to Buckingham Castle is much different from the gallows?" she asked.

"I do not plan to take you to either. But if you do not stop kicking me, I will leave you in the middle of the woods and let you take your chances with the wildlife." Not a terrible idea since she was probably safer with a starving wolf than a hungry duke.

"Why would you help me?" Why indeed?

"Because Jimmy, a young boy living at Trent Castle, seems to think you are a hero. Smart lad but quite misguided." Let her keep her disguise. It would be quite fun to torment her male counterpart.

"Is Jimmy   " Lady Georgiana cleared her throat and deepened her voice, "—safe?"

"Delivered him into his grandmother's arms. He asked me to save you. So, here I am. And my thanks is that you try to render me incapable of satisfying a lady."

She gasped.

"Thankfully, I am gifted in that department so it will take more than a foot to my balls to dampen my skills."

Too bad she could not see his charming smirk.

"Get off of me!"

"If I get up and untie your hands, will you behave?"

She grunted.

"I find you a comfortable mattress indeed. I can stay here for a very long time. Of course, I imagine there is a lot of body weight on your wrists." His sigh was the height of Shakespearean drama. "I also suppose your back is cold from lying in the muck."

"Fine," Winkentattle said.

"*Fine,* what?" William asked.

"I will behave."

"Promise?"

"Yes."

"An honorable *man* keeps his word."

"I bloody well said I would behave. Now let me up," she said.

William took his time standing, helped her to her feet, and reached for the burlap.

"No!" She bristled. "I will remove the hood myself."

He prepared for her attack as he worked at the bindings on her wrists. Once they were loose, instead of punching him, she turned her back and squatted. The moonlight silhouetted the removal of her hood. He squinted as she shoved long strands of hair under her wig. When she stood, something fluttered to the ground.

He bent to retrieve lace and wet paper. "What is

this?"

She grabbed the paper and fabric and tossed them into nearby bushes. Then she stomped on the burlap.

"We need to get going," William said.

"Trent Castle?"

"Why would you want to go to Trent Castle, *Winkentattle*?" William asked.

"*Umm... I...*"

Suddenly, he was too tired to toy with her. "I do not know where we are going."

Where in God's name could two aristocratic traitors go? Holy hell, he did not want to go to the continent.

"But we cannot stay here, we will freeze to death," he said as he climbed onto Lightning.

She waved off his assistance and mounted behind him. Her breasts pressed against his back. Even after the hell they had been through, she maintained her scent of lavender and roses.

He clicked his tongue and headed southeast in search of warmth.

Chapter Twenty

December 29th, 1816

Baron Goldcount growled. For in the middle of the pasture stood thirty cows wearing his brand-new cravats.
From Tattle's Tales

Georgie closed her eyes and sunk into William Harrington's warmth. The mesmerizing rhythm of the horse's hooves and the rocking in the saddle lulled her into a dreamlike state. The longer she rode, the less the chilly nip and fear bothered her.

"Whoa, Lightning," William said.

Georgie opened her eyes. Here and there, a gas streetlamp burned, and stucco and timber buildings lined a quaint village street.

"Where are we?" she asked.

"I am not sure, but I think that is an inn." William pointed at the most prominent structure.

No matter how hard she squinted, Georgie couldn't decipher the words on the wooden sign waving in the wind.

"Stay here. I will make sure it is safe," William said.

The second he leaped down, she shivered. It was as if her body craved his nearness. Or maybe she temporarily required his body heat. Either way, she was not taking chances.

"Two rooms," she called using her Winkentattle voice.

He disappeared into the dark.

Maybe this was all a dream.

She pinched herself. "Ouch!"

No such luck! She was in serious trouble. At least keeping her masculine disguise in place would prevent her from behaving like a simpering fool around her rescuer.

Since horses made wonderful confidants, she leaned forward and whispered, "Lightning, I have been so foolish. Christopher and Peter were correct. I am nothing but a naive foolish woman who has endangered people with my radical ideas."

Lightning whinnied.

"I know. But I have no idea which regiment converged on us or if Stephen is safe."

Lightning shifted his weight.

"And William Harrington—how can you stand him? The man is infuriating. All he does is strut around and laugh at me. And currently—" She sighed. "Well, currently, I am not in the mood for his nonsense, seeing as how I may find myself headless at any moment."

William reappeared and sauntered toward her, carrying a lantern. Her death was imminent, and the man pranced. He kissed the gelding on his pretty black snout. Georgie's silly girl parts tingled.

"The innkeeper and his daughter have heard about Winkentattle's arrest. They have not heard anything about the Duke of Astleyshire helping Winkentattle escape. If we do not call attention to ourselves, we should be safe until morning. I will take Lightning around to the stables in the back." He handed her the lantern. "Sneak to the third floor, the last room in the hallway."

Georgie dismounted and followed his directions.

The room was small but cozy. The contents were minimal: a bed in the center of the room, a single nightstand, a fire in the fireplace, and a basin holding an empty pitcher.

Georgie stripped off her coat and held the lantern up to the mirror above the washstand. Ghastly. Her mustache tilted to the left, giving her a deranged smile. Some of the soot she had coated her face with still remained, making her resemble a filthy waif. She tucked wayward strands of hair under her wig.

Without warning, William entered, carrying an oil lamp that he placed on the nightstand. He flung off his coat, sat on the bed, and thereupon, stripped off a boot.

"What are you doing?"

"I do not plan to sleep in my boots?"

"You cannot stay with me. I told you to get two rooms."

"I heard you. But we are safer together. If it bothers you that much, you are welcome to sleep in the stables. Let me warn you, I saw a rat." The man shivered, then smiled.

Someone knocked on the door.

William motioned for her to hide in the far corner. "*Shh,*" he said as he limped across the room on one booted foot. He waited for Georgie to squat behind the bed before cracking the door.

"Thank you, Amy," he said.

"Can I get you anything else, Richard?" a young-sounding female asked.

"This is perfect."

Amy giggled like an absolute fool.

The door closed, and William Harrington grinned over a tray of ale, bread, and cheese. He met Georgie in the center of the room and handed her a pitcher of warm water and a small dish of soft soap.

"Richard?" she asked.

"Well, I sure as hell could not tell her I am the devil of a duke that will soon be notorious for betraying his country."

Georgie stopped short, her jerky movements sending the water splashing down her front. Might William Harrington be headed to the gallows with her?

"You can wash first. Just save me some warm water." William shoved a hunk of bread into his mouth, placed the tray on the bed, and plopped down beside it. He swallowed. "What are you looking at?" No sooner had he spoken, and his mouth was full of cheese.

The most heroic, handsome man in the world satiating himself as if he had not partaken in a year.

She gave herself a light tap to the cheek, grounding herself. Washing her face might remove the dirt, hair, and pitch, divulging her identity, so she left him what she hadn't spilled down the front of her. Sitting on the opposite side of the bed from him, she glowered. "You only got one drink?"

He handed her the cup. "I intend to share. First, it will soon be dawn, so we were lucky to get anything. Second, I did not want anyone to know I have a companion."

She chugged. Not that she often imbibed, but the brew was not half bad.

"Save me some."

She swirled what was left and handed it back. Waving off golden brown bread she asked, "What will we do?"

"I need sleep. I am certain the answer will come to me in the morning." He tossed down the rest of the drink and shoveled in another hunk of cheese. "Are you done washing?"

She nodded.

His lips curved, straightened, and curved again. "Winkentattle, your face is covered in dirt. Quite repulsive. Good thing we are not trying to find ourselves a half dozen doxies this evening. For, I would surely have them all, and you would have none."

Georgie's cheeks and temper caught fire.

William wrestled with his other boot, stood, and stretched. Then, he did the unthinkable—he took his time unbuttoning his shirt.

Georgie inhaled, a pathetic impression of a male Winkentattle gasp.

William flung his shirt to the ground and sauntered to the washstand. The firelight dappled over his sculpted back muscles. Georgie looked away, and fiddled with her mustache as she studied the counterpane.

"Hey, Winkentattle," he called.

"What?"

"My good man, I will sleep closest to the door."

Both Georgie and Winkentattle were speechless. The water splashed.

"*Mmm, ahh...*"

Georgie peeked out of the corner of her eye. William made absurd sounds as he lathered up and scrubbed under his armpits and across the double swell of his firm pectorals.

"Oh, that's nice," he said.

Did all men moan and groan as they washed?

William grinned as he strolled to the bed. He plopped down, stretched out, and put his arms behind his head.

Dear Lord. Georgie struggled to breathe.

"Hey, chap, please blow out the lanterns before you come to bed."

Inhale. Exhale. Inhale. Exhale.

William locked his gaze on hers. In the firelight, his pupils were almost black, and his eyelids drooped. "Are you staying up all night?"

Georgie had no choice but to crawl off the bed, turn down oil lanterns, and snuff the rushes. She tossed a scoop of coal onto the fire and stared at what was left of the bread and cheese. Then her gaze drifted to William Harrington. His legs were too long for the mattress and his biceps cradled his face.

Georgie was so tired that she sat on her side of the bed, fumbled with her boots, and kicked them into a corner. She checked to ensure her hairpins were in place and gave her wig a tug. Please let it stay in place if she tossed and turned.

Fully clothed, she lay next to a man who was not one of her brothers. She did not give two shites about propriety. Still, she couldn't do this. Sleeping beside a duke who made her feel strange sensations could not happen.

She would tell him the truth. Then he would understand why she needed her own bed.

"William," she said, her voice soft and feminine.

Too late. The Duke of Astleyshire snored twice before rolling onto his side and placing his back to her.

Bloody hell! It would be a long night.

Chapter Twenty-one

December 30th, 1816

Baron Goldcount would not be humiliated. He ran around that pasture retrieving each and every cravat.
From Tattle's Tales

William awoke with a throbbing bulge squashed in his pants and a filthy-faced woman poking him in the bicep. Using a hand, he shielded his eyes from the light streaming in through the window.

"Hey, Astleyshire, are you awake?"

He moaned. "How in the hell did your face get dirtier overnight?"

"I have no idea what you are talking about." Winkentattle needed to work on his indignant look, seeing as how the chit had left a trail of ashes from the fireplace to the mattress. "Get up. We need to talk."

"Give me a minute," William said as he tried to talk his cock down.

"We need to free those prisoners. Immediately."

His cock instantly deflated. Problem solved.

William sat up. "What in the deuces are you talking about?"

"We cannot let the villagers hang. They were only standing up for what they deserve."

"There are two of us. There were at least nine

soldiers guarding them."

"Well…" Winkentattle worried her pretty, plump, soot-covered lip. "I can take on five of them if you can handle the other four."

"Absolutely not. If I do not figure a way out of this mess, I am probably joining you on the gallows."

With the sagging of her shoulders, the spitfire was gone. "But if they die it will be my fault."

Those intoxicating, green eyes would be the death of him.

He sighed. "I have no idea how to find them."

She gracefully leaped out of bed. However, a second later, she clutched her ribs and moaned.

"Are you hurt?" he asked.

"I am fine." She grabbed her boots. "And if you will not help me, I will find them without you. I am sure I can handle nine men." The little minx peered out the corner of her eye at him. Her gaze slid to his bare chest, and she looked away.

Despite her gawping, sex was probably out of the question. "Can we at least get something to eat first?" he asked.

"Yes. But hurry. I need a horse, and we both need weapons."

****

Winkentattle rode a brown gelding she named Burney. A shiny, sheathed sword hung at her waist.

William also sat atop a horse with a beautifully crafted weapon by his side. However, he had additional frills. There was a pistol shoved into his garters, his skirts were hiked up so that he could straddle Lightning, and a ridiculously large bonnet did not keep his wig in place.

Winkentattle laughed so hard she snorted.

At least he did not have a begrimed face and locks held in place by so many hairpins it had to be excruciating. No indeed. His blond strands were blowing about freely.

"You are one ugly woman, Your Grace," Winkentattle said.

William *harrumph*ed. "You are one scrawny *man*." And one hellishly beautiful woman.

Winkentattle composed herself for a second before chortles again shot through her.

"Control yourself. Or you will fall off Burney and knock yourself out cold."

Winkentattle sat tall, exhaled, and exchanged mirth for a serious expression. "Did you learn anything?"

"According to Amy and her parents, a traveler said he passed the prisoners outside of Letchworth, and Winkentattle was on his way to London with the Duke of Astleyshire."

Winkentattle cringed. "So, word has circulated?"

"Hence my quick visit to the brothel to purchase a disguise."

The lady blanched.

"Do not worry I paid the ladies well," William said, swathing her with his practiced pompous-ass smirk.

"How long until we catch up to them?" Winkentattle asked.

"They are about seven hours ahead of us and we can travel twice as fast. If we make haste, we should head them off by early evening. "However—" William swallowed. "I do not want to injure soldiers doing their jobs. I know one brave soldier in particular…"

"Do you mean Stephen Eaton?"

"Yes." Although they might not have contact with the 1st Life Guards, reminders of her twin might temper Georgiana's impulsivity.

"I do not want anyone to die," Winkentattle said.

"Maybe you should have thought about that before you incited chaos."

She paled and accidentally used her feminine voice. "I know."

He cut his gaze to her, and an arrow shot right through his heart. This brave, headstrong woman stood up for her beliefs even if it meant risking her life, and he would never take that from her. Instead, he would protect and support her, all while making sure no one lost their life.

"Come on." He clicked his tongue, squeezed his heels into Lightning, and they were off.

Seconds later, the woman who had turned his world upside down caught up, and then overtook him.

Chapter Twenty-two

December 30th, 1816

Jackson Valiant fluffed both his long wig and his décolletage, then fluttered his lashes at the smitten baron.
From Tattle's Tales

What a fine disguise she wore. Her alter ego had caused untold problems and did nothing to protect her from the blue eyes messing with her resolve.

The pink rouge smeared into his cheeks, red lip salve coating his lips, unfashionable purple bonnet and tight cloak did not make William Harrington any less appealing—perhaps because she now knew the man beneath the costume.

He could hide behind the garb of a prostitute or his normal arrogant manners. Neither changed the fact that, like Alistair, William was loyal to his family, he was as charismatic and popular as Evan, and he equaled her twin in bravery.

Additionally, William oozed common sense. At first, she argued when he said they had to stop for an hour. However, there was no denying that the horses required rest, she and William should eat and replenish fluids, and they needed a plan.

They sat in the dark corner of a pub, hardly

conspicuous—an ugly woman and a scrawny man, partaking of an unpalatable mutton stew and warm ale while whispering secrets.

"Once they reach Newgate, we will not be able to help them," William said.

When she straightened William's wig, her finger brushed his cheek, eliciting exciting tingles. She dropped her hand.

William's breath hitched. Clearing his throat, he backed away. "I will order another pint and two more bowls of stew." Wearing the largest pair of slippers in the world, he tromped to the bar, practically plowing down everyone in his path.

She giggled. What poor prostitute had feet and clothing that large because the duke made one masculine, giant woman.

Then she sobered. How foolish of her. He was obviously distraught, thinking that a man had touched him with too much affection. If she told him the truth now, would he ever forgive her? Could she breathe if he left her alone and aching for his touch?

Enough was enough. She needed to control her mawkish emotions.

A balding whippersnapper followed William.

William leaned across the bar and spoke to the tavern keep.

"Nay, he is not—"

As she predicted, the man grabbed William's bottom.

How dare he treat a lady—even a pretend lady— like that. Georgie was by William's side in an instant. She tapped the drunk on the shoulder.

"What do you want?" He turned and squared his

shoulders to her. "Aren't ye a sight to behold? A dirty-faced flapdoodle thinking you can satisfy me lady." The man tugged William to his chest.

William shook free of the man's grasp and held up a palm to Georgie.

The duke could act as if being the object of a man's piggishness was not a big deal. But Georgie would not ignore it. "Apologize to the lady."

"Why don't we let the miss decide who she'd rather be with." The man grabbed his crotch. "Lassie, me prick'll make ye scream with pleasure."

William rolled his eyes. His voice high, he said, "I chose the man I came with." He reached for Georgie.

The ratbag growled and formed a fist, but since he was uncoordinated from drink, she would knock him on his arse before it reached her nose.

Instead, William intercepted the punch and grasping the man by his collar, shoved him as if he weighed nothing.

The drunk landed back first on a table, taking out a half-dozen mugs.

"What the bloody hell?" yelled a mustached man with ale dripping down his forehead.

Large hands grasped Georgie. She turned to find the barrel-chested tavernkeep. He lifted her off her feet.

"Do not think of coming into my establishment to cause trouble."

"Put him down!" William's voice had become a threatening baritone.

No sooner was she dropped onto her feet when an uppercut caught her square on the jaw. A blinding pain seared her brain. She yelped and rallied. First, she kicked the tavernkeep in the stomach. Her next kick

153

met the mustached man's chin.

Fists, chairs, and obscenities flew from all directions. In her peripheral, William tossed men as if they were snowballs.

"Get to the stables," he yelled while jabbing his elbow into a man's nose.

She punched, kicked, and shoved her way toward the exit.

William had only made it halfway across the room when the door banged, and Redcoats entered. Georgie's hand grasped the hilt of her sword as she scanned the room, searching for a back door.

"Do not do it," said a voice that sent shivers up her spine. "Hands above your head."

No. Dear God. She spun to face green eyes.

"Georgie, what the blazes?" said her twin.

Her moment of hesitation allowed two soldiers to take her to the ground.

"Georgiana!" William yelled.

A foot stomped on her face and her world went black.

****

"Georgiana. Georgiana," someone cooed.

And then there was nothing.

A flash of light, then darkness.

Thirst. Unrelenting thirst! So, so thirsty.

PAIN!

Pitch-black nothingness.

****

"Georgiana, please wake up."

Georgie fought with her eyelids until they opened. A blurry William Harrington looked down at her as he cradled her in his lap.

"Georgiana. Oh, thank God." He caressed her cheek. "You scared me to death."

"Newgate?" she croaked.

"No," William said, "the local gaol. We were accused of starting the tavern fight. You were knocked out and have been asleep since."

Georgie struggled to sit. The room spun. Mutton and ale filled her esophagus. She pushed from William's hold to retch in the corner of the musty cell. The light of dawn filtered through a window at least three feet above them and an elderly gray-haired man slept in the opposite corner.

She collapsed onto the dirt floor and dropped her forehead into her palms. William curled up beside her and wrapped her in his arms. When she looked up, William's countenance reflected concern. His purple dress was torn and caked with dirt.

"Stephen was one of the soldiers," she said.

"Are you sure?" he asked. "I did not see him, but it was mayhem."

Georgie nodded. "He recognized me. He even called me by name." She caught William's gaze and searched his soul. "You also just called me by name."

He twirled a strand of her hair between his fingers.

"Oh, no." She patted her head.

He chuckled, removed her wig from his pocket, plunked it on her, and shoved her hair beneath it.

She sighed in resignation. "When did you know it was me?"

"The second I saw your eyes on that stage." He shrugged. "And you smell of lavender and roses."

"And you let me—" The effort it took to indignantly wave her hands about required more energy than she currently had. They dropped to her side. "You let me make such a fool of myself."

His breath brushed her cheek, and his voice was soft. "You are far from a fool, Lady Georgiana Eaton."

Her gaze slid to the sleeping man, and she whispered, "You let me sleep beside you."

"Yes." His lips brushed her cheek. "And it was sweet torture."

If overwhelming physical need constituted *sweet torture*, then indeed it was.

"William?" she whispered.

"Georgiana…" He cradled her face in his hands and kissed an eyelid.

She whimpered.

His lips traveled over her cheeks, bestowing a dozen gentle kisses. "Does it hurt?"

Pleasure shot through her.

"You have a cut on your face, the beginnings of a black eye, and there are bruises on your torso from where your captors kicked you."

She tilted her head, allowing him to trail those decadent kisses down her neck.

"Please forgive me. I only looked so that I could assess your injuries," he said.

How could she have ever found him vexing?

It was hard to tell where the pain from her beatings ended and the ache of raw desire began. Perhaps making love in a cold prison was wrong, but his ministrations eased all forms of agony. Besides, she might not have much longer to live. If Winkentattle was not beheaded, she would soon have typhus from the draft.

"I do not know how to kiss a man," she confessed

as she threaded her fingers through his hair and pulled him to her. Parting his lips with her tongue, she entered his mouth.

He did not seem to mind her inexperience because he moaned as his tongue tangled with hers. He pulled back, ripped the mustache from her, then tossed it across the cell.

"You are so bruised, I do not want to hurt you," he said, his voice and touch so gentle he could not have hurt a flea.

"Please," she begged. "You make all the pain go away." She pressed her body to his, soaking up his warmth.

Something clanged, and they both jumped. The cell door opened, and three men with masked faces entered.

"Who are you?" William demanded.

They tore Georgie from his grasp.

"No!" She reached for William.

"Let go of her." William attempted to stand, but the butt of a pistol smashed him in the back of the head. He crumpled to the ground.

"William!" Georgie punched and kicked as the men dragged her across the floor.

"My lady," one of the men whispered. "Please stop. We don't want to hurt ye."

"I want to bloody kill you!" She grunted at her captor before her teeth latched onto his ear.

"Bollocks!" He let go of her to wipe away the blood.

"She is as fiery as a surly wasp," said one of the men.

They had no idea!

Chapter Twenty-three

December 31st, 1816

"Such a lovely bosom." Baron Goldcount salivated as he leaned close to the luscious lips of the large lady and puckered up.
From Tattle's Tales

When William came to, the sun blasted through the small window and the old man in the corner stared at him. He placed one hand over his nose to block the bitter effluvia as he rubbed the tender spot on his crown with the other. The shooting pain caused him to grumble a string of expletives.

"Why are ye wearing a dress?" the old man asked.

William waved him off and plunked his now scraggly wig on top of his sore spot. "'Tis a long story."

"We got time. Lots and lots of time. All the time in the world."

William was not feeling patient or amicable, so it took a lot of effort not to throttle the man. He rose and teetered unsteadily. Thereupon, he paced.

Lots of time his arse. He was getting out of there if he had to break down the door. With each trip across the cell, his anger increased, and his strength returned.

He halted in front of his cellmate and gagged as the smell of urine burned his nostrils. "Do you know who

158

took my companion?"

The man tapped a finger to his wrinkled brow. "The funny-looking chap you were boohooing over?"

"Patience, Harrington," he mumbled under his breath.

"Ye don't gotta go getting all lippy with me." The man rubbed his eyes and refocused on William. "Are you one of them men who likes men?"

"Do you know who took my friend or not?"

"Or not," the man said. "Ye got any gin with ye?"

"I think you have had enough." So much that the drunkard sat in his own urine.

The man crossed his arms over his chest and closed his eyes.

A panic like he had never felt shot through William, and he flung his body weight against the cell door. There was no way he could budge it, but smashing something provided a much-needed outlet for his anger. He charged again.

"Let me out of here. Now! You bloody bastards!" His fists pounded again and again.

"*Shh*. Ye'll wake the dead," said a muffled voice from outside the cell.

William halted his barrage and stepped back.

The door opened and the masked men from earlier entered.

"Keep it down, or you'll stir the guard," one of the men said.

"And let's be quick," another said. "He's gotta come around soon, and then ye are in deep shite."

"Where is my companion?" William asked.

"She's safe. Are we gonna have to knock ye out to get ye out of here?" The tallest of the lot waved a bludgeon. "I have always wanted to hit a duke."

William held up submissive hands. He would strangle the men later. For now, he would do whatever was required to get out of there and find Georgiana.

****

The inn sat in a wooded area outside of town. The small room was windowless and dark. However, the fire was warm, and the blanket wrapped around his shoulders was soft. William sat beside Georgiana as their rescuer plied them full of water, currants, and apples and listened to their adventures.

"Harrington, I apologize again. I had no idea you were with my sister," Stephen Eaton said.

"They beat him with the butt of a pistol," Georgiana said.

The captain sighed and ran his hand through his red hair.

"They dragged your sister out by her armpits."

"I could not free you myself, and the men I hired are a bit rough around the edges." The captain leaned back in his chair. "I simply told them there was a lady dressed as a man being wrongly held captive."

Georgiana crawled onto her twin's lap. She wobbled as she wrapped her arms around his neck. "Thank you."

"You are down to one sideburn, and you have a black eye." Stephen exhaled, then steadied her as he held her close. "I love you, Georgie. So much so that I have risked my reputation and future."

She touched each of her cheeks, wincing as her fingertips traveled over the left side of her face. "I know. I am sorry."

"And Astleyshire, I am speechless. I thought

Winkentattle was your enemy."

William drummed his fingers on the table. "I was protecting Georgiana."

So much for the affection the lady had recently shown him. She again glared at him like he was the King of Fools. "I do not need your protection."

"Enough, Georgie," her brother said. "You do not need protection because you are a woman. You need it because you are impulsive and reckless."

William ran a hand over his jaw. "Captain Eaton, I am of the opinion that Georgiana is right to draw attention to the factory conditions. Do you know how many of the workers are dying from tuberculosis?"

Georgiana's countenance softened, and her luscious lips parted.

"But Astleyshire, these things need to be handled in Parliament, not by riding around England starting fistfights."

"Parliament?" Georgie *harrumph*ed.

"I agree with you, captain," William said. "And I have an idea."

Stephen placed his hands on Georgiana's hips and removed her from his lap. "I have been away long enough. My men will worry. My sister is now your responsibility." He held up his palm, halting his twin's protest. "Georgiana Eaton, do not make me drag you back to Alistair and Grandmother. I am sure they are losing their minds with worry."

Georgiana looked at her boots.

"Do you know where our horses are?" William asked.

"Are you headed to Trent Castle?"

"Yes," William said.

"They are in the stables out back. Leave by the backdoor. Once the guard awakes and it is discovered that you are gone, there will be a search for you. I am unsure of the loyalty of the ruffians I hired or the silence of the innkeeper. I paid well, but if someone is willing to pay more…"

"But they do not know who we are, correct?" William asked.

"They have no idea that the tavern brawlers are the Duke of Astleyshire and Lady Georgiana Eaton." Stephen cringed. "Or Winkentattle. You are simply two troublemakers who rode into town. If they figure it out, the bounty on your heads will be high."

The twins hugged and William clasped Stephen's hand. "Thank you. I owe you my life."

"I owe you for saving my sister's life."

The door clicked into place behind Stephen.

William gazed into those green eyes. "Would you like to hear my idea?"

"Yes. Later." She opened the door a crack, peered after her brother, and counted to thirty. "Come on. We need to find new weapons."

Thereupon the stubborn woman disappeared into the hallway.

Chapter Twenty-four

December 31st, 1816

Maria Seraphina snuck up behind the two men, winked at Jackson Valiant, and smacked the baron over the head with a chamber pot.
From Tattle's Tales

Georgie used her time in the saddle for introspection. Once she freed the individuals she felt responsible for, Winkentattle was no more. Although her intentions had been noble, her methods were irresponsible. She had not helped a single person and left untold chaos in her wake. She fought tears as they rode hard and fast, chasing an elusive caravan.

Unfortunately, William Harrington galloped behind her, shouting at her back.

"This is too dangerous, Georgiana. Your family has to be worried. Do you not see how responsibility has aged Alistair? Your poor grandmother. She will break a hip if she continues to suffer with her vapors. Think of young Jimmy. He looks up to you. Are you not concerned that your noble brother has risked his reputation and commission for you?"

Of course, she was concerned. Her thumping heart threatened to burst through bone, muscle, and skin.

Lightning cut off Burney, and William blocked

Georgie's path as he stared into her soul. "Listen to me."

"I hear you!" Every single cautionary utterance.

"Damnation! I could not take it if anything happened to you."

Unable to remain stoic for one second longer, Georgie's tears flowed, dripping down her cheeks and coating her chin.

Finally, after hours of William's flaring nostrils, his tense jaw softened. It only took her complete breakdown to bring out his compassion.

Georgie looked away to dry the tears on her sleeve. "Help me do this one last thing and I will go home and put Winkentattle behind me."

"This one last thing will get us both killed."

"Do you not understand? I have messed up so terribly." More tears tumbled. "All of those people— men and women, some not much older than Jimmy— will die because I encouraged them to fight. I told them if they banded together, they could not be defeated."

"Georgiana…" His lips quivered.

"'Tis true, and we both know it. How will I ever live with myself?"

He sighed, turned Lightning toward London, and dug his heels into the gelding's flanks.

****

Dusk had fallen by the time they reached the outskirts of London. Georgiana was about to accept they were too late when she spotted the caravan parked in the distance. The fading sunlight and a half dozen carriage lamps combined strength to illuminate two wagons and four horses.

Georgie and William pulled into a clearing to

whisper.

"You ride up ahead and create a diversion. While the men are dealing with you, I will free the prisoners," Georgie said.

"That is an excellent plan," said someone from behind them. "And absolutely no one gets hurt."

Georgie held her breath as she looked over her shoulder.

A man wearing rags sat on top of an exquisite Pinto, whose brown mane blew majestically. Green eyes peeked out from above a piece of fabric tied around the newcomer's face.

She was lucky she didn't topple off her mount. "Stephen, what are you doing here?"

"*Shh.* You two are as loud as an animal circus at feeding time." He glared at her. "My dear stubborn sister, I knew you would not listen, so I am here to keep you safe."

"I tried to stop her," William said. "I considered tying her up with the rope and then tossing her over my shoulder."

She gasped as his words shot tendrils of pleasure through her.

William sighed. "Instead…"

He undid the cloak around his shoulders and looked down at his nonexistent cleavage. Seconds later, the fabric was waded into a pillow and shoved into his dress. He fluffed up his absurd breasts, jumped off Lightning, and grinned.

"How do I look?"

"You are the largest woman I have ever seen," Stephen said.

Georgie struggled to take in the entire disguise

since she was focused on those twinkling blue eyes and perfect masculine lips. Stephen dismounted and righted William's wig. Before dashing into the woods, William swung one of the bundles of rope over his shoulder and handed Stephen his pistol.

Georgie slid off Burney, and they tied the horses to a nearby tree. Thereupon, she and Stephen tip-toed closer and found a large oak to hide behind. Georgie crouched so that they could watch William's show from the same side of the tree.

He stood in the center of the road wearing one slipper. "Please help me. I was out for a walk and lost my shoe." He lifted his skirts to display a well-formed calf.

It seemed William Harrington had forgotten to purchase a full set of women's sit-down-upons.

"*Bluck*," spat Stephen. "If it were not so dark, I bet we could see ruddy black hair. And that voice could split an eardrum."

This was no time to giggle. Georgie bit down on her index finger.

"I think my slipper might be over there." William pointed toward the woods. "But I do not have a candle. Could one of you help me?"

"There is no way they are falling for this," Stephen whispered.

William turned to the side and pushed out his ample cleavage.

Stephen moaned. The scene was much too entertaining for Georgie to express indignance.

One of the soldiers strutted right into the tree line. Swinging his hips and blabbering away, William followed.

A moment later, William reappeared. He smiled at one of the guards, struck a pose that highlighted his endowments, and crooked a finger. "Could you fetch more light? 'Tis so dark, we can barely see, and my slipper is stuck under a branch."

A second soldier lit a candle on one of the carriage lamps and strutted to William.

"Oh, you are indeed helpful boys," squawked William.

Knowing the Duke of Astleyshire, he was probably fluttering those bewitching lashes.

"Men. Fools. The lot of you," Georgie said with a self-satisfied smirk.

Stephen cringed, his protest noticeably absent.

William emerged from the trees, waving his hands. "Help! Please help. A tree covered with snow fell on them."

Another soldier marched to William's rescue.

"Unbelievable," Stephen said. "I pray my men are not this gullible."

He could pray all night. Large breasts tended to addle men, leaving them mutton-headed.

"That leaves six men," Stephen whispered.

"I gotta find me a tree," said a handsome soldier with blond curls as he trotted into the woods.

Georgie held up five fingers.

Stephen handed Georgie William's pistol and removed his from its holster. "Do not shoot anyone and keep your sword sheathed."

He need not be so bossy. She didn't plan to shoot anyone. As for her sword...

Once they flanked the men, Stephen whistled and five soldiers wearing terrified expressions snapped to attention.

"Zooks," said one.

"Bamboozled by a homely woman," said another.

Served them right for being lecherous.

Using his pistol, Stephen herded the soldiers into a small group. "His voice threatening, he said, "If you want to live, do not make a sound. This lot of traitors is not worth losing your life over. Place your weapons in front of you and step back."

Not one man argued.

Winkentattle kicked pistols and swords to the side while calming the hooded captives in the wagons. "Please remain quiet so that we may free you without incident."

Their murmurs and gasps halted.

Stephen handed Georgie his weapon and unwound the rope. Back stiff, he approached the soldiers. Georgie kept both pistols aimed at the party.

"Face the wagon and sit," Stephen demanded.

The men followed every directive. When the blond returned from relieving himself, Georgie moved the gun in the direction she wanted him to travel.

"Move slowly and place yourself with the others," she said.

Wearing two slippers, William exited the woods and aided Stephen. They had the soldiers bound in no time. It really was quite impressive.

Then, while Georgie and William removed the hoods and untied the Crown's prisoners, Stephen intimidated their captives with his squinted eyes, wide stance, and the pistols aimed at their heads.

"You are not far from London." William handed out the discarded weapons. "You have been saved from the gallows, so do not cause any problems. Find a place to warm up and then head to your homes."

After releasing the prisoners, the trio hastened to their horses.

"We did it!" Georgie clapped.

"I knocked two of the men unconscious." William frowned. "They will have headaches when they come to. The third is tied up and has a piece of my skirt shoved into his mouth."

"But we did it," Georgie repeated.

"You will head home now, Georgie?" Stephen asked.

"Yes." Oh, to take a bath, and get rid of the lone itchy sideburn. And she wanted to don a silk dress. What was William's favorite color?

She blinked until the absurd sentiment dissipated. "I promise." She wrapped her arms around her twin and kissed him on the cheek.

"I am glad you got rid of that ridiculous mustache." Stephen chuckled as he mounted and rode off.

Georgie and William's gazes met, and he rubbed the back of his hand over his mouth. Was he thinking about kissing her with that silly caterpillar above her lips?

"Let us go," he said.

They mounted their geldings and to Georgie's surprise, William aimed Lightning toward the city.

"Where are we going?"

"*Shh,*" he said. "They will free themselves quickly and we do not want to be followed."

Georgie's mind whirled as she and Burney kept pace with Lightning and William. Surprisingly she felt relief instead of disappointment about not wielding her new sword. Well, relief mingled with fantasies about silk dresses and William Harrington's lips.

It was time to give in to her desires. Perhaps her dangerous dash across the country had reset her priorities. And if she ever got the chance to sleep beside William Harrington again, she would do it as a woman.

Then reality knocked the wind from her. She and Stephen had remained anonymous, Winkentattle would simply disappear, and Stephen would find his regiment and carry on as if nothing had happened.

But the Duke of Astleyshire remained an enemy of the Crown.

Chapter Twenty-Five

December 31st, 1816

Baron Goldcount licked his lips. "Yum, honey." He tiptoed up to the beehive.
From Tattle's Tales

William exhaled relief. This must be what a sailor docking experienced after eons at sea.

Newly installed gas lights in front of Rosa House served as a welcoming beacon. The five stories of his Mayfair townhouse made it the tallest on the street, and a balcony resplendent with intricate stonework perched majestically over the main entrance.

A bittersweet heaviness settled over William because the platform that sat off his bed chamber had once belonged to his parents.

His party passed the house on their way to the stables.

Not wanting to startle Johnston, Rosa House's head groomsman, William knocked on the stable door and cleared his throat before entering.

Still, the poor man jumped. "Your Grace!"

With Georgie and the horses at his heels, William traveled to the groomsman.

"Your Grace. I am so glad to see you." Johnston lowered his voice to the decibel right above a whisper.

"But soldiers are looking for you. They say you helped a prisoner escape."

"My good man, 'tis a long story. Hopefully, all will be right by tomorrow evening. But no one can know I am here. I need everyone to use the greatest of discretion."

"I will see to the horses." Johnston's gaze traveled over William as he schooled his features, not reacting to the wig, too-tight coat, torn dress, or large filthy slippers.

The next stop was in the kitchen. Mrs. Kingston, the longtime head housekeeper, brought a hand to her mouth. "Your Grace! What the dickens?"

Cook simply stared.

He hugged both women, lavished their cheeks with kisses, then pointed at a one sideburned, mustacheless Winkentattle. "Meet Lady Georgiana Eaton."

"What the dickens," Mrs. Kingston said again.

"Our visit must be kept a secret," William said.

Both women nodded.

"But, Your Grace, we did not expect you so soon after your last visit. Rosa House will not be fully staffed until your return in February," said the frowning housekeeper.

"So much the better." William was still learning how each of his properties was staffed. "Is Buttons here?"

"Yes," Mrs. Kingston said. "Johnston and Anna are also on staff. Everyone else is at Hockley Castle until Parliament is in session."

"Perfect," William said. "Cook, could you prepare us something to eat right now?" He bonked the stern woman on her nose with one of the flirtatious love pats that made her cheeks redden and her eyes sparkle. "Simple is fine. And we will dine at this table." He indicated the surface the food was typically prepared on.

Cook stared at the table and cringed. "Of course, Your Grace. Right away."

"Mrs. Kingston, could you fetch Buttons and Anna and ask them to come to the kitchen."

Mrs. Kingston curtsied and left.

William pulled out a chair for his guest. She hesitated, bit her lip, then sat.

Placing hot tea and biscuits on the table, Cook said, "I don't got nothin' fancy, Your Grace. Just what is left from our dinner."

"That will be fine."

"It ain't proper for me to be servin' a lady biscuits and beef stew."

Georgie shoved half a biscuit into her mouth. "I wuv biscuits and beefth stew," she said, her mouth full.

William chucked. The woman was beyond divine.

The young inexperienced butler and even younger maid followed Mrs. Kingston into the kitchen, their steps hesitant and their eyes wide.

"Please sit," William said.

The staff joined them at the table.

"This is life and death. No one must know we are here."

Everyone but Georgiana nodded. She was inhaling biscuits.

"Mrs. Kingston, please put Lady Georgiana in my sister's room for the evening so she can use Katrina's bath. I will use the bathing chamber. Make sure we both have a fire in our rooms. Anna and Johnston can help.

Buttons, word must be sent to Lord Trent that his sister is safe. Pay well for discretion. No one is to know she is here, just that she is safe."

Cook set two bowls of steamy stew on the table.

Georgiana pulled her dish close and blew. They had not had much sustenance the last twenty-four hours, and the poor woman, with her insatiable appetite, was obviously starving.

"Anna, please go to my father's study and gather writing paper and pens and bring them to me after my bath."

"Yes, Your Grace." The girl looked at her feet. "'Tis now your study."

"Remember, no one is to know we are here or to disturb us," William reminded them once again before dismissing his staff to attend to their duties.

****

A clean-shaven and freshly scrubbed William tapped on the chamber door. "Lady Georgiana?"

No one answered.

After her warm bath, she had probably fallen asleep. As much as he wanted her to rest, they had things to do. His scheme had to work. One night in a local gaol had almost done him in. He would not survive locked in a cell at Newgate.

He cracked the door and peeked into the room. The fire cast a warm glow over the decadent wallpaper and ornate furniture, and a tallow candle flickered from the nightstand. However, the bed was empty.

He placed the paper and writing instruments he carried on the nightstand and retrieved the candle, aiming it into the far corners. A faint light filtered around the door of the private bathing chamber. He closed his eyes and listened—a raspy moan and his whispered name.

His heartbeat picked up. Georgiana was in trouble and she needed him? Her next utterance let him know that she did indeed *need* him and his balls tightened to an excruciating level of delicious pain.

He should walk back into the hall and wait for her to dress because even though this beautiful virgin was exploring her pleasure, she deserved a gentleman.

Unfortunately, he found it impossible to be gentlemanly when a woman cooed his name between breathy sounds. Besides, she could pretend that she did not want him, but at last, the undeniable truth was out.

He stepped lightly and peeked into the private chamber.

Most of Georgiana Eaton was submerged beneath the water. But her pale shoulders, two bruises, and the swell of her bosom sat above the water line. Condensation from the steam danced over her skin and shimmered in her hair.

Her eyes were closed, and her head rested on the rim of the cast iron tub. Two fingers skimmed over a nipple. The other hand disappeared beneath swirling flower petals. She undulated. Water, rose petals, and William's cock all stirred.

"William," she whispered, still unaware that he was there.

To hide and watch this siren forever, or move closer? Candle in hand, he pushed on the door and stepped into the room.

She gasped, sat tall, and hid her exposed torso beneath crossed arms.

"Do not stop," William commanded.

Her lips parted, and her gaze pinned him in its wake as he placed the candle on a dressing table that held a row of flickering wicks. He pushed aside a pink dressing gown and night dress and plunked onto a chair. If she threw him out, he would die from the ache.

"Georgiana, do not stop." Desperation and raw need oozed from the command.

Holding his gaze, she licked her lip and leaned back.

"Yes," he murmured as he opened his thighs to accompany his growing cock.

As her palms traveled over her shoulders, her eyes pleaded for his approval.

"Yes," he said. "Let me see your breasts."

The headstrong woman had been replaced by the seductress that hid in that luscious body. She caressed herself with slow circles before holding her palms beneath the plump mounds and lifting them above the water.

"Beautiful."

Those pink nipples were probably as soft as the petals giving off the intoxicating sensual scent.

"Can you feel my lips suckling?" He taunted them both. "You taste of strawberries and sweet cream."

She tilted her head back and gasped. He fought his urge to dive in and drown in her scent, taste, and feel. But the sight and sound of her were too delicious for him to move.

"Georgiana," he whispered.

Although her eyes opened, her lids hung heavy over emerald eyes.

He let his gaze fall to the depths of the tub. "Touch yourself again."

Her forearms disappeared, and she quivered.

"Christ." He sat forward. "My darling, you are so tight, and warm, and inviting."

"Ohhh," she moaned.

"Let me in deeper."

Her hair flew as her head oscillated from side to side.

"There is that sweet bud. Can you feel my fingers stroking it?" His cock throbbed.

"Yes," she said, her voice husky.

He growled as he imagined her pearl pulsing and quivering.

She writhed and bucked. "William!"

Water splashed onto the floor, as he clenched his entire body to keep from coming inside his buckskins.

Even though her body relaxed against the side of the tub, and she closed her eyes, her breaths came hard and fast until they eventually evened out and softened.

Composing himself, he carried her a towel. She stood and water droplets cascaded down her figure.

"Damn."

So many conquests over the years and not one with her perfect mix of firm muscle and soft curves.

She shivered. He wrapped the towel around her. One arm tucked under her knees and the other cradled her back as he lifted her from the tub. She snuggled against his chest as he carried her to the bed. Not wanting space between them, he reluctantly set her down. His gaze slid to the blank paper on the nightstand.

If he buried himself inside Georgiana Eaton, he would remain there until the soldiers came and pried their naked bodies apart. But it would be worth it to hear her call his name as he came deep inside her.

Except he would prefer to make love to her forever. He needed to show her his beloved Hockley Castle and to stand on the front balcony of Rosa House and look out over Mayfair with her by his side.

He met her heated gaze. "Georgiana, please get dressed. We don't have much time."

She sat up so quickly that her towel slid down, exposing those decadent fleshy mounds. "I-I…"

He reached an arm toward her, pulled back, then dashed into the hallway, slamming the heavy door that was the only barrier between him and the woman that would surely be the death of him.

Chapter Twenty-six

Midnight, New Year's Eve, December 31st, 1816

Baron Goldcount's arms flailed about as he ran around the garden, slapping the buzzing bees from his face.
From Tattle's Tales

Georgie sat on the edge of the bed as the red-hot sear of humiliation started in her stomach and traveled upward, exploding from her eyes and lips in tears and a groan.

What had she just done? She had read of such things in a scandalous book that Evan had accidentally left in the library. But to actually engage in the act?

She whimpered.

There was only one solution to her debacle. She would borrow a dress, shoes, and gloves, and hail a coach headed to Trent.

She wrapped the towel around her and padded to the wardrobe. Anna, the pretty maid, who blushed every time the duke came near, had told her to help herself to any dress she wanted. Apparently, Lady Katrina Harrington was both spoiled and generous. As if that combination existed.

"Wait."

Georgie caressed a simple but elegant violet dress.

Her father and brothers spoiled *her*. And she was generous. She sighed.

Lately, the barrage of shades-of-gray logic had her befuddled.

She opted out of stays but slid into silk stockings, garters, and a chemise. The soft violet tumbled over her, and the hem landed with a graceful *plink* at her ankles. The matching slippers were a bit tight, but she could handle the chaffing for the time being.

Sitting at the dressing table, she searched through Katrina's belongings, settling for a vigorous hair brushing and loose locks. She grabbed a dark purple pelisse, bonnet, and gloves, blew out the candles, and headed for the chamber door.

Her palm on the handle, she halted. It was the middle of the night. And how would she pay? Perhaps Johnson would take her to her family's London home. From there, her brother's staff would help her.

She opened the door and ran headfirst into a hard-as-brick wall of duke. His strong hands steadied her as he inhaled.

"*Mmm*," he murmured. "I can still smell the roses."

The tingle in her body picked up exactly where it had been when he left her naked and aching. She attempted to push past him. "Excuse me, please."

He grasped her forearm. "Where are you going?"

"Not that it is any of your business, but I am headed home. I am sure my family is worried sick."

"I sent word to them."

She tried again to step around him.

He lifted her chin gently, forcing her to meet his gaze. "After everything we have been through, you would leave me to the gallows?"

Those bloody blue eyes.

She swallowed. Even if he rejected her a million times over, she would protect him until her dying days.

His arms were around her, holding her so tightly that she could not break from his grasp even if she wanted. She inhaled citrus and cedar as the bulge in his pants pressed into her. He wanted her as much as she wanted him. Anger and humiliation *whooshed* out of her with a sigh.

"You will get me out of this the same way you got me into it," he whispered into her ear.

She pulled back to gaze into his eyes.

"Write me out of this predicament, my darling Georgiana."

"What?" Her palms pressed against his strong chest. "I do not understand."

"Our dear prince does love a good story," William said with a wink.

****

The next day, Georgie awoke on the velvet settee in William's study. The new year's first sun filtered through the windows, casting glistening rainbows over William's forearms and profile. He chuckled and set down the paper in his hand.

"Is it funny?" she asked.

He smiled. "'Tis, my darling. How did you sleep?"

She had only gotten a few hours of sleep, but it had been more fitful than the past few evenings. She stretched like a satiated feline.

The door to the study opened. Anna and Mrs. Kingston entered, carrying trays.

Georgie sat up, sniffed, and her stomach gurgled. She followed the scent of eggs, bacon, sausage, tea, and honey to William's desk.

He pulled a chair beside his and indicated she should sit. "I asked for breakfast to be brought to us so that we could continue working."

"What a splendid idea," she said. "Please tell Cook it looks delicious."

"Of course, my lady," Mrs. Kingston said.

"Please call me Georgie," she said, her mouth already full.

She did not miss the secret glance between William and the wide-eyed housekeeper.

"'Tis fine, Mrs. Kingston," William said. "Georgie is not a fan of class distinction."

A bite of eggs halted halfway to Georgie's mouth. William had called her Georgie. He had called her infuriating and vexing, and most recently darling. Georgie sounded divine coming from his lips.

The staff curtsied and left Georgie and William to their food and writing.

"What do you think?" Georgie inclined her chin toward her story.

He waved a piece of bacon about. "Brilliant. But could you make the prince more virile?"

She nodded. "I think so."

"He must be more handsome and appealing than Valiant."

It would be a challenge, but she could write anything she set her mind to.

William held the honey cake beneath his nose, inhaled, and moaned. "Write something about Goldcount stealing from the king."

Georgie could not begrudge the sweets for occupying his attention. One bite and her mouth watered. She sipped tea and devoured cake as she considered what Goldcount might be stealing.

"Money, jewels, women?" she asked.

William looked her in the eyes, leaned close and whispered, even though there was no one there to hear. "Handershane is charging the prince four times more than he charges his other buyers."

"No!" She slammed a palm on the desk and the teacups rattled. "Scandalous. How is he getting away with that?"

"He has also almost doubled taxes on his tenants without having it approved by Parliament."

She choked on her tea. "How do you know these things?"

"The prince himself sent me to find out who Winkentattle was?"

Georgie knew it.

"I thought Evan was writing the chapbooks."

She set down her fork. "Because you did not think it could be a woman?"

"Until I met you, I thought women had no interest in such things."

She bit her lip.

"And at the time Evan and I shared no love for the other."

Georgie stiffened. "I know you cheated at cards and slept with the Widow Hemmingsworth." She could not look him in the eyes. "And Evan wanted her."

"I did not cheat. However, I was so foxed I could barely walk so I probably could not see the cards. And as for the widow, nothing happened between us that night." William grasped her hand. "Georgie, I showed up at Trent Castle under the guise of finding

Winkentattle. I thought that Evan was the traitor. Instead, I came to respect your brothers and adore Jimmy. And Handershane is a swine. Not only does he steal, cheat, and lie, but he told one of the young girls in the factory that unless she slept with him, she would lose her job. There are probably dozens of women in the same predicament."

Georgie brought a hand to her mouth.

"I met you and have been a bumbling fool ever since." He squeezed her palm, and her thighs trembled. Leaning close, he kissed her.

Georgie pulled away before she crawled onto his lap and begged him to make her feel like a sensual woman. "How long do we have?"

"I have sent a missive to ask for an audience this afternoon."

She shoved a piece of bacon into her mouth as she gathered the story from William's desk. There was no time for dawdling and kissing.

She had mere hours to save the man she loved.

Chapter Twenty-seven

January 1st, 1817

The welts covering the baron's face and arse hurt like bloody hell. He'd had enough.

"Today you die, Jackson Valiant and then I shall climb on top of Maria Seraphina and claim her as mine."

From Tattle's Tales

William paced from one end of his study to the other. A still-as-a-statue Georgie sat on the floor near the fire, her legs crossed, and her eyes closed. There was no need for words. Sexual attraction, affection, and fear mingled, swirled, and crackled.

Finally, Buttons entered carrying a silver salver that held a white card.

William rushed to him, grabbed the missive, and read it twice.

"What does it say?" Georgie asked, her eyes now wide.

William strolled to her. "We have much to discuss. Please come at once, for I leave for Brighton tomorrow morning. Your affectionate but confused cousin, G PR." He extended his hand and pulled Georgie to standing.

Georgie had chosen her outfit with care. Her thick

185

hair hung loose, landing below her shoulders. She wore a tight green vest that matched the color of her eyes and buckskins that hugged her curves. Her bountiful cleavage swelled from above the vest, showcasing her feminine assets. Although face powder did not completely conceal her black eye, she was one hundred percent seductive female in shocking power clothing and expensive riding boots.

William pulled her into his arms and kissed her forehead. "My darling, you will charm the prince to his core, and he will want you for his very own."

Georgie Eaton, the male-hating spinster, pressed her body against his. "Mayhap, but I prefer my dashing duke."

William chuckled as blood pooled in his cock. If he did not soon bed this delight, he would lose his mind.

****

William and Georgie sat in a gilded room. The cost of the ceiling ornamentation alone might feed the starving waifs they had ridden past on their way to the castle for a year.

Why were so many children clad in tattered threads roaming the streets? Perhaps William would toss his coat to an indigent youth on the way home since he was sweating more than the corpulent man beside him.

Pastries of every size and color filled the platters on the side table.

The prince partook of a pink cake while perusing Georgie. He washed the treat down with a sip of tea and turned his attention to William. "Despite the reports, I knew you had not forsaken me and escaped with a traitor."

"As you can see, Winkentattle is not an enemy of

the Crown but a high-born lady who loves her country." William's upturned palm showcased Georgie. "I was certain you would want me to deliver her myself."

Georgie graced his cousin with a devastatingly charming smile. "Your Royal Highness, I know you are a great patron of the arts, and I would be most honored to read you this last edition as a gift. I wanted you to be the first to hear it."

The prince extended his hand, inviting her to stand.

She obliged and pulled her shoulders back. Before she could utter a word, the prince said, "My lady, you resemble a nubile female pirate I once saw in an opera."

She did indeed resemble a beautiful buccaneer, but now was not the time for William to nurse an erection. If he were alone on the high seas, he would pin her beneath him on the deck and tell her just how desirable she was.

She grinned. "You flatter me, Your Royal Highness."

William's disheveled hellcat had become all sophisticated, sensual allure. Perhaps he had a hand in the transformation? Whatever the reason, he planned to enjoy her many charms the second he was exonerated.

His plan had to work. He had a dukedom to run and a woman to love. If he failed, he had placed the woman who had stolen his heart in grave danger. His gaze slid to Georgie. He drew in her essence and knew without a doubt that they would succeed.

Georgie cleared her throat and embodied the deep timber of Winkentattle.

The prince tilted his ear toward her and listened attentively. He slapped his thigh with glee. "The daft fool seems to find manure wherever he goes."

Halfway through the tale, the prince scowled. "Goldcount is maggot pie."

Georgie proved a master thespian, acting out an energetic fencing scene as she read. Meanwhile, the prince cheered with every parry and thrust.

The battle scene over, he waved a hand and bellowed, "Someone should hang Goldcount the cockchafer."

William chuckled. If the queen heard her son use such coarse language, she would swathe him in her terrifying glare and take away his iced cakes.

Georgie, her features and movements animated, wound up for the plot twist.

"Then, with his foot on the deceased Goldcount, Jackson Valiant told Maria Seraphina his greatest secret. 'My lovely Maria, I am your prince in disguise. I did all of this so that I could fight at your side and rid the world of jolterheads like Goldcount, for I love you.' "

The prince regent brought a hand to his heart and gasped.

"Then Jackson pulled Maria into his arms and their lips touched. 'I love you, Jackson. With all of my heart. Forever and ever.' "

"Bravo." The prince peeled his bulk from the chair to stand and clap.

Georgie bowed, then sat with her hands folded in her lap.

"It was a wonderful story, Georgiana. Or should I say, Winkentattle?" The prince winked. "I do love Jackson and Maria." He sighed. "The name Maria reminds me of someone I once held dear. And you have given the prince such admirable characteristics. But I can see why Baron Handershane is concerned. Goldcount does share similarities and I understand you appeared in Trent Village—"

While the prince coughed, William held his breath, and Georgie worried her pretty lip.

A servant handed the prince a silk napkin. He wiped the spittle from his chin and, at long last, continued.

"—His Majesty's army intervened before any equipment was broken, but many suggest your acts were traitorous and had anything been destroyed, you might now be in Newgate awaiting execution."

William sat forward. "But nothing was destroyed. I understand there were only minor injuries. You entrusted me to find answers. I investigated Winkentattle, the Eaton family, Baron Handershane, and his factory. And cousin, I found a charming woman fighting a tyrant with her gift for words and a repugnant factory owner whose mistreatment of workers is leading to deaths and injuries. He is abusing his position to sleep with young girls. Not only this, he is raising the taxes on his tenants without the permission of Parliament." Sweat dripped into William's eyes as he sought courage. "Sir, even though you gifted him with a title, he is charging you four times as much as his other buyers."

The Prince Regent choked, and his pastry landed at William's feet.

****

William sat with his thigh touching Georgie's as their carriage headed to Rosa House.

"Oh, William, he wants me to write more stories about Jackson and Maria. And they will be distributed to both the working class and the elite." She wrapped her arms around her chest, swaying as she hugged herself. "As G.E. Winkentattle."

William grinned. "I knew you would charm him. We simply had to tame the feral cat and replace her with a swashbuckling seductress."

Georgie playfully slapped his shoulder.

"Ouch." He rubbed out the non-existent sting.

She tapped a finger to her cheek. "Still, I must find a way to intertwine women's rights and social justice for all in these tales."

"My darling, I would be disappointed if you did not."

Georgie stared at his mouth as she ran her tongue over her top lip.

He schooled his moan, but it did not keep the swell in his lap from growing.

Unfortunately, his evening plans had gone awry. He had intended to ravage his pirate princess. But the prince had pulled him to the side and whispered, "I do hope you plan to marry our Lady Georgiana since you have deflowered her."

William did a double take. "I have done no such thing." Yet.

"That is not what Thomas Merrick said. He claims you bet him one hundred pounds that you would bed the lady in one week."

William did not give a shite about the money. 'Twas the damnable ungentlemanly bet that bothered him. He had worked hard to push the bloody Marquess of Birmington's son's haughty chuckle and shite-colored eyes from his mind. "How did you know that?"

The prince pointed to the other end of the castle.

"*Ton* gossip does not escape my mother's ears."

Now, unable to take Georgie's scalding heat one second longer, William put distance between them. He needed to climb into a freezing tub immediately. Yes, that was the solution—his nether regions ensconced in ice until he had properly proposed to Georgiana Eaton.

That is, if she did not get word of the wager and run a sword through his heart.

Chapter Twenty-eight

January 1st, 1817

With Goldcount defeated, the villagers rejoiced as their heroic prince paraded through the streets, Maria Seraphina by his side.
From Tattle's Tales

Since dinner at Rosa House was a joyous occasion, Georgie borrowed an emerald and silver gown, and Anna pulled her hair into a lovely updo. Soft curls framed Georgie's face and diamond hairpins glittered throughout her copper strands.

William wore a royal blue waistcoat and cravat, and the collar of his fine shirt had been starched to frame his chiseled jawline.

Mrs. Kingston clasped her hands in a prayer position. "Never have I seen such a lovely couple!" she exclaimed upon their entrance into the dining room.

The silver had been polished to perfection, and the fire cast a warm glow over the light blue upholstery and wall coverings. Not a single bite of duck or dumplings went to waste. Georgie even indulged in a glass of rich port.

Everything was perfect except that William sat at the opposite side of the large table, and they had to yell to be heard.

Georgie formed her hands into a cone that projected her voice. "Come sit beside me," she called.

Her heart took flight at his sparkling eyes and spectacular grin. With drink and baked custard in hand, he settled beside her.

Laughing at their siblings' antics and bittersweet memories of past holidays with their parents consumed the next two hours.

Eventually William sighed. "Georgie, I think we should turn in for the night."

"Yes, William," she said, her voice gravelly.

"It will take us at least two days to travel, and we want to make it in time for your grandmother's Twelfth Night Ball."

For the first time in her life, a ball sounded festive. "Will you dance with me?" She aimed for a coquettish shoulder lift.

"Only if you promise not to separate my limbs from my body." He smirked.

"I do so like your limbs, so you had better behave."

Perhaps she had finally learned the art of flirtation and crawling into bed beside the duke was the most delightful of propositions. When he caressed her bare skin, and she cried out her pleasure, she would finally be his woman.

"I shall do my best to behave, my darling." He chuckled, then sighed. "Mrs. Kingston and Anna shall help you prepare for bed."

She nodded.

"Anna will travel with us."

No! "Why?" The beautiful woman's eyes lit up too much in William's presence.

"Because 'tis not appropriate for you to be

traveling alone with me. Being in the house is improper enough, but at least the staff is present."

How utterly absurd. They had been alone together for days. "But William—"

He held up a palm. "We were on the run and feared for our lives before. Now we are safe and comfortable."

His warm fingers tilted her chin upward and his lips brushed hers. As he lingered, a hungry heat overtook her.

When he pulled away, his lids hung heavy over darkened eyes. "Mrs. Kingston, Anna," he called.

The women must have been lurking right outside the room, because they appeared instantly.

"Please, help Lady Georgiana pack an overnight bag before her bath. Anna, you will be accompanying us. We leave at dawn."

"Wait," was as much protest as Georgie got out before William strutted from the room.

"Mrs. Kingston, I will not require warm water for my bath this evening," he called over his shoulder.

****

Georgie left her chamber door unlocked and dumped petals into the tub. Then she took forever to bathe, lathering a translucent bar of garden-scented soap into her skin. The water eventually chilled her bones.

William did not come.

She spritzed her body with rose water, applied a vermilion pomade that added a soft sheen to her lips, a light rouge, and dressed in a lavender night shift.

Still, no William.

Sliding into slippers, she grabbed a candle and tip-toed to the library in search of a book. Hopefully, she encountered her confounding duke during the trek.

Minutes later, she returned to her chamber clutching *The Memoirs of a Woman of Pleasure* by John Cleland. Her curiosity was piqued years ago when her father removed the copy from his library because her brothers had gotten into a fistfight over it.

And here it was, just in time. Hoping to learn how to satisfy a man, she cuddled up in bed with tantalizing literature.

...storms of kisses...unabated fevered exercise till dawn of morning...firm texture of limbs...square shoulders...

How absolutely scandalous.

...compact hard muscles...

Whimpering, her palm brushed over an aching breast.

She dropped the book onto the mattress so both hands could explore. "William, where are you?"

Her touch left her wanting, so she groaned into the counterpane. After tumbling from bed and not bothering to put on slippers or a night wrap, her bare feet stung as she padded down the cold hallway to William's chamber.

She tapped. There was no answer. She grasped the handle, preparing to enter. Before she could push, the door opened a crack.

The Duke of Astleyshire was only partially dressed. His shirt hung open exposing his neck, chest, and abdominals.

She swallowed.

"Georgie, what the blazes?"

He peeked out around her, then pulled her into his chamber. The door clicked into place, and he backed her up against the hardwood.

"What are you doing here?"

The potency radiating from the man scorched and enticed.

When she placed her palms on the *compact hard muscles* of his chest, his heat scorched to her core.

"You did not come to me. I waited and waited." Like a child with a sweet—or a wanton woman—she could not control her impulses. Her nails raked through his chest hair.

He hissed and grasped her hands, halting her exploration. "I wanted to. But, please understand that I cannot. I have behaved in a most ungentlemanly manner. I need to seek Alistair and ask for permission—"

"Nay, William. You must ask *me* for permission. And I want you to touch me."

His unseemly "Fuck" tickled her from her heart to her toes.

He let go of her hands to place a palm on either side of her head, trapping her against the door. As if one could imprison an enthusiastic visitor. His breathy words caressed her cheek.

"My darling, you will be the death of me yet."

With her hands now free, she explored his torso, her fingers dancing over his muscled chest. "Does this feel good?"

"Amazing." His gaze pierced blood and bone to reach her soul.

"William, please kiss me."

He pushed her against the door and threaded his fingers through her hair. Georgie met his need with her own. Like their swords had fought for dominance a few days ago, their tongues engaged in a sensuous battle. Needing more, she pressed her aching breasts against him.

His lips traveled down her neck and across her shoulder as he freed her from the nightdress. He stopped kissing her to stare at her breasts. "Christ!"

Georgie waited for a sensual assault as the tips of her nipples reached for him. Instead, he clasped her face in his hand and stared into her eyes.

"What is wrong?" she asked.

"I foolishly let myself be drawn into a bet."

She bit her lip as her heart crashed.

"I was foxed and in a foul mood and allowed the Marquess of Birmington's son to bait me. I bet the arse one hundred pounds that I would bed you within one week."

She detested Thomas. No way would she allow him to take this night from her. Besides, everyone knew the marquess was a swag-bellied fool.

"I dare say, you have lost one hundred pounds," she declared.

William's handsome face contorted in confusion.

"For it took you eight days to bed me. Eight glorious days. And eight is one more than seven. And there are seven in a week, but—"

His lips crashed against hers. He picked her up and carried her across the room, tossing her onto the bed. He flicked his shirt off and it fluttered onto the carpeting.

She propped herself on her elbows and licked her lips as he slid his trousers to his ankles and kicked them into a corner.

He stood before her fully naked, the firelight

highlighting the contour of his sculpted body. As inexperienced as she was, she knew desire made his member reach for her. And he was hers—a-statue of-a-Greek-god-duke—whom she wanted right this instant.

"Now, make me feel like a woman for I am tired of being a silly miss," she demanded, her voice husky with need.

He pounced, his body weight caging her beneath him. "A woman?" He smirked. "Thank deuces, I know exactly how to do that."

She closed her eyes and inhaled his scent of cedary citrus. Each touch and every kiss elicited a lightning-like spark. His lips traveled over her shoulder to her breast, and he suckled.

"Ohhh." How delightfully naughty. "Ohhh," she murmured again, her other breast aching for the same attention.

"William…"

"My darling?"

She guided his head to her lonesome nipple and his lips, tongue, teeth, and hands languidly doled out pleasure. Then, his ministrations traveled down her torso.

She writhed and her thighs dampened.

William's breath blew across her hip. "Do you feel like a woman yet?"

It took effort to focus her lust-filled eyes. William grinned up at her from between her thighs.

"Yes."

"Good." His deep voice landed heavily in her pelvis. "But I am not yet done."

What the? "William, no!" she cried out in shock as his tongue dipped into her feminine folds.

He pushed her thighs wide, and his tongue delved deeper.

"Yes! God, yes." Hips bucking, her fingers threaded through his hair, and she held him against her intimate area. She needed his tongue, his face, his body, his heart, all of him, inside her.

He lapped, drinking her pleasure as his moans vibrated her insides. She shivered and trembled. Her thigh muscles tensed to the point of pain, then an unbelievable pleasure knocked against her secret places.

She begged shamelessly. "William, please."

His thumb and index finger joined his tongue. A swirling touch. A pinch. Pressure. Then, an explosion. The tension released, and she soared.

William crawled up her body to gift her with a sweet, musky-tasting kiss. "I think you might enjoy this next part even more."

"'Tis not possible." She caressed his cheek.

"We shall see." He guided his tip to her opening. "This may hurt. But only for a moment."

She braced for a pain that never came. Instead, torrential pleasure coursed through her as her walls sucked him deep. Crying out in pure rapture, she wrapped her ankles around his back and met his thrusts.

"Deeper," she begged.

He grunted and slammed his hips against hers.

"More," she cried.

His jaw tensed and his lips parted, and oh, he was glorious. She tugged him close for a kiss. The second their lips touched, he grunted, and his body quaked.

As his warm seed shot into her, she sang out, "William!"

For a long moment, their panting was the only sound. Finally, he dropped onto the bed beside her and wrapped her in his arms.

"I love you, Georgie, my darling. Please be my wife."

"If you will be my husband." Her lips cupped his ear. "And I love you more than honey cakes, my dashing duke."

Chapter Twenty-nine

January 2nd, 1817

Maria's handsome prince pulled her into his arms and kissed her until she saw stars.
From Tattle's Tales

Georgie visited William's dreams. She enticed him to a sensual fencing bout that ended with her straddling him. Then naked, she crawled into his bathtub and gently washed his back. On a bright summer day, they snuck off into the gardens at Rosa House and made love in a half dozen positions beneath the trellis. And finally, while in a warm bed, she ran a searching hand down his torso to his pelvis, and his cock grew hard beneath her caresses.

He had not had so many damn wet dreams since he was a man of ten-and-eight.

"William," a soft voice cooed. "Oh, William. Wake up."

He opened his eyes to find his lady's hungry gaze devouring him.

"I like this." She dropped her focus to his erection.

"Me too."

Her finger brushed the tip. "Does it feel good when I touch it?"

"That *it* is named *My Grace*." He chuckled.

Nicki Pascarella

"Good morning, *My Grace*." She grinned wickedly, then licked along his entire length.

He closed his eyes and reveled in the ecstasy as she experimented and explored. Touches here. Kisses there. Licks at strategic locations. And then, with one breath-stealing suckle, she pulled his length into her mouth. In and out, she guided him with the skill of one experienced in such things. He could take it no longer. He grabbed her and pulled her on top of him.

"*My Grace* would like to go for a morning ride."

"I would be delighted."

Together they pressed his cock to her opening and sunk him deep.

"That is it, my darling. Ride me." He cupped her breasts as she undulated.

She threw her head back and moaned.

The woman made up for her inexperience with bold passion. Had he known how thrilling athletic women were, he would have abandoned sedentary females long ago.

Her strong thighs pressed against his hips, and her walls squeezed and pulsed around his cock. If she did not slow down, he would erupt like a randy youth.

"I am going to come," he said.

"Yes," she murmured with that sensual resonance that drove him wild.

He clenched his jaw, wrapped his hands around her waist to hold her in place, and fought his orgasm.

"Please," she begged.

"Too soon." He panted.

She leaned forward, clasped his bottom lip between her teeth, and bit down.

"Fuck, Georgie," he cried as wave after wave of

pleasure spiraled through him and he came deep inside her.

While his body melted into the sheets, she hovered over him and grinned. "Shall we have breakfast and then do this again?"

He chuckled and ruffled her hair. "We must be on our way."

"Not until we have filled our bellies and made love everywhere." She grasped his hand and tugged him from the bed.

Her firm round buttocks, curved hips, and shapely legs distracted him from further protests.

"How about right here?" She spun to face him, her countenance all mischievous enchantress.

Before he could answer, Lady Georgiana Eaton knocked him onto his arse in front of the warm hearth.

"I win," she said as she straddled him and climbed onto his once again stiff cock.

Let her think that she had won. Seeing as how he was balls deep in the woman he craved more than air, he was the hands-down champion.

****

Luscious extenuating circumstances meant they were still in William's bed late into the afternoon and he had never experienced such blissful peace or sensual pleasure.

Georgie's head rested on his chest. Her gorgeous red locks spread out around them as she traced lazy figure eights over his pectorals.

"May Millie come to live with us?" she asked.

"Of course."

"I will miss Jimmy, and Cook, and Mrs. Teague." She held up her hand and ticked off her fingers. "And

Chester, Oliver, Alistair, and Evan. I already miss Stephen." She sighed. "I would like to visit Trent Castle often."

"Of course," he said.

"I will read, write, and fence every day."

"I hope so."

"I want a puppy."

"We shall have a litter," he said.

Her soft laugh vibrated his chest.

"Georgie?" He lifted her chin and lowered his so they gazed into each other's eyes. "Do you think Jimmy would be happy at boarding school?"

Georgie sat up.

"Do you think a young boy could be happy if he was not with his own class?" William leaned against the pillow. "I could hire the best tutors to get him ready. And eventually, I could send him to university. I know he will want to spend his holidays with Alistair and his grandmother, but perhaps he could stay with us for a fortnight during the summer."

She wrapped her arms around his neck and kissed him. "Oh, William. Let us ask him."

He nodded. "I have been thinking, and…"

Her expression invited him to continue.

"I am concerned about the number of children in the streets. 'Tis winter and they do not have coats. Perhaps I should set up some sort of aid society."

"Oh, William." A tear trickled down her cheek.

"I am sorry. I did not mean to make you sad."

She wiped away the rouge droplet and ran a hand along his cheek. "There are horrific tales of what orphaned children endure living on the streets."

"I will take this up with Parliament. That, and the

conditions in the factories. I fear something must be done about these things."

Georgie clapped as she bounced on the mattress beside him. "I love you so very much." She settled on her buttocks, tapped a finger to her chin, and graced him with her impish grin. "I dare say, I have not yet had you in your study."

Why, the little minx.

She flew from the bed to wrap herself in his robe. "Last one there is a rotten plum," she called over her shoulder, as she took off into the hallway.

Laughing, William left his warm bed to dress. "*I* have not yet had *you* on the balcony, the stables, under the trellis, on top of the dining room table…"

He was still talking to himself, listing the places he planned to make love to his lady when he caught up to her.

A naked Georgie sat on his desk, swinging her feet. "Come here, rotten plum."

He slinked to her.

It was settled. Before the afternoon was over, his soon-to-be duchess would cry out his name in every nook and cranny of Rosa House.

Chapter Thirty

Jan 5th, 1817

Maria Seraphina lifted the wedding veil from her face and smiled.
From Tattle's Tales

It was early afternoon when Georgie and her party entered the stables behind Trent Castle. Oscar greeted them and relieved them of the horses. Georgie wrapped the beloved groomsman in her arms.

He allowed her to hold him tightly and only pulled away when she had finished absorbing his warmth. "Your Grace, my lady." Always dutiful and affable, he bowed and then smiled at Anna. "The countess and the earl are losing their minds with worry."

Georgie exhaled. William's comforting palm rested on her shoulder. Anna, who had proven herself a devoted companion, clasped her elbow and they strolled to the center of the room.

"The stable looks fuller than when I last saw it. Have guests arrived?" William asked.

Oscar nodded. "Lord and Lady Davenport, the Doolittles, and Baron Killian and his family will be staying for a few days and have settled in."

Georgie shuffled her feet. They had dallied too long at Rosa House—although it had been divine. Still,

Alistair would bellow until her ears bled and the countess would require a barrel of smelling salts.

"We aren't expectin' the rest of the guests for a few hours, so if you make haste, you'll be ready in time." Oscar ran his hand over Burney's snout. "And who is this fine fellow?"

Georgie introduced Oscar and Burney. Thereupon, leaving out the most scandalous details, she provided the groomsman with a recap of their adventures.

"My, what a time you had," he said.

"We had better go." Georgie inclined her chin in the direction of the house and whimpered.

Oscar leaned close to whisper, "Good luck, my little Georgie. Do not let anyone break your spirit."

They were halfway up the front steps when Millie exited the great house and wrapped Georgie in her arms.

"I missed you so much. We received word that you were safe, but we were still so worried." She warily eyed the duke as she cupped Georgie's ear. "I watched from the trees as they arrested you. I tried to come to your rescue, but Christopher held me back. He said there was nothing I could do."

"The Duke of Astleyshire came to my rescue." Georgie peeked over her shoulder at him and grinned. "Of course, I did not need rescuing."

He winked, and her heart pitter-pattered.

"How vexed is the countess?" Georgie asked.

"Do not worry about that. You know she loves you." Millie bit her lip.

"What weighs on you, Millie?"

"After Jimmy returned from the protest, he told Alistair everything. He was not betraying you. He had no other choice."

Although she agreed, Georgie cringed.

"But Georgie, somehow, he already knew."

Alistair knew? And he had not tried to stop her? What an enigma.

"And the countess told me that she began to suspect when she threw your chapbook in the fire, and you looked as though you might cry and you never cry," Millie said. "Plus, she recognized your writing."

Tarnation.

"Did Evan know?"

"He did not until Alistair told him. He is glowing with pride. Strutting around saying, 'Why, my big sis is a rebel-rousing chap.'"

Georgie's heart warmed. Her baby brother was about to receive a hug that would squish his insides out his ears.

With William and Anna at their heels, Georgie linked arms with Millie, and they entered the house.

Alistair and Evan stood in the foyer.

Alistair's scowl only lasted a moment before he grinned like a fool, grabbed Georgie, and hugged her.

Evan hauled her off her feet and spun her in a circle. "Not even His Majesty's army can stop my sister." He set her down and glared at William.

"Please do not be hard on William. He put himself in harm's way for me." Stephen's role in her plight was a secret she would take to the grave.

"Georgie!"

Jimmy dashed toward her. Two balls of fluff scampered behind him.

Georgie squatted to wrap Jimmy in her arms. "You got your puppy?"

While the puppies ran circles around them, barking, Jimmy hugged William around his thighs. "Your Grace."

William ruffled the boy's hair. "Hello, Jimmy. What did you decide to name them?"

Jimmy peered upward, his eyes full of affection for the duke. "My puppy is the one with the stripe on his nose. His name is Duke. He is going to be a sheep herder."

The pup seemed to know his name because he leaped about until the boy scratched him between the ears.

"But there are two puppies," Georgie said. Please let the golden pup with one floppy ear be hers.

Alistair folded his arms across his chest. "If you had not run off you would have had her a few days ago."

"She did not run off. She was arrested." Evan's grin was absurdly toothy. He picked Georgie up and spun her again.

She chuckled as the world whizzed past. Evan plopped her onto her feet and lightly punched her shoulder. Laughing, she punched him back. A game of Eaton punchy punchy broke out.

Jimmy interrupted their childish shenanigans. "I have been calling her Lady."

"Lady it is." Georgie scooped up her bundle of joy and kissed her on the nose.

Jimmy inclined his chin to Anna.

"Jimmy, this is Anna. She is one of the maids at my house in London." William pinned Alistair in his gaze. "She has acted as a companion and a chaperone to Lady Georgiana."

Alistair showed no emotion. But Evan sucked on his jaw.

William's gaze slid back to Jimmy. "Would you like to show Anna Trent Castle?"

Jimmy's face lit up and he grabbed Anna's hand. "Come to the kitchen and meet my grandmother. She is the cook. We get to taste the food for the ball and tell her if it is good and 'tis always good. Come on, Duke," he called over his shoulder.

Duke trotted after the pair.

The dowager countess clicked into the foyer, and her eyes widened. She dropped into a curtsey. "Your Grace."

Georgie held her breath and waited for the epic Crash of The Countess.

"Georgiana, I hoped you would make it home in time. I had Millie prepare your gown. If you start preparations, you should be ready to greet our guests." Nervous energy radiated off the woman as she tapped her foot.

Overcome with emotion, Georgie clutched the old woman with one arm and held her puppy to her chest with the other. "Hello, Grandmother. I know your ball will be perfect."

"Oh, Georgiana." Tears dripped down the countess's cheeks. "I was worried, and I missed you so very much." For the first time ever, her grandmother kissed her on the cheek. "Let me help you pick out the perfect jewelry. Come to my chamber, and you may have whatever you want." She grasped Georgie's hand. "And the Christmas gift you painted hangs above my bed. It looks lovely. You must see it."

That was about as shocking a declaration as

Georgie had ever heard

She was dragged away from her fiancé and her frowning brothers.

"Duke, you have some explaining to do," Evan said.

"I hope I do not have to challenge you to a duel." Alistair growled.

"Or slice off your balls," Evan said.

Georgie gasped and halted.

"Men." Her grandmother rolled her eyes. "Do not worry. There will be no duel or chopping off of body parts. 'Tis simply a case of men and their bravado. And I know you would never have engaged in impropriety with His Grace."

Neither of them seemed convinced of the countess's last statement since they both cringed.

Thereupon her grandmother tugged Georgie up the grand staircase.

Chapter Thirty-One

Jan 5th, 2018

"Now, kiss me, my handsome husband, then let us be off, for I hear there is a tyrant in Deene who needs to be taught a lesson."
Jackson and Maria mounted their geldings and rode off into the sunset.
From Tattle's Tales

William stood amongst a group of the *ton*'s eligible bachelors. While the men perused the room in search of the most beautiful and least troublesome women, William only had eyes for the lone redhead awkwardly staring at her shoes. She would never fit in with this ostentatious crowd that was part of their world. And he would trade every second of their admiration and favor to spend his life in her arms.

"Arabella Beaumont is quite handsome. But I dare say, a dance with her would leave one feeling rather like an ugly mole rat," Lord Kingsley said.

"Especially if one truly is a bald, pink rodent," declared the conceited Thomas Merrick as he infiltrated the group.

The men, minus William, chuckled. It was not that he did not find humor at Kingsley's expense, but he had no desire to speak to Thomas Merrick while looking down the man's toothless gullet.

Georgie wore a golden gown that emphasized her ample cleavage and shimmered and sparkled as the hundreds of diamonds embroidered into the fabric reflected candlelight. Despite her desire to remain plain, she was the most beautiful woman in the room. Her younger brother sauntered to her, handing her a drink.

They sat on a bench beneath a glowing apple tree and partook from the plate he held. The dowager had outdone herself creating a whimsical orchard and her grandchildren sat amongst the finery, whispering and giggling. Even from across the room, Georgie's genuine smile knocked the wind from William.

At one point, Georgie punched her brother in the arm, and the pair doubled over in laughter.

Lord Kingsley crinkled his face in disgust. "I see that Lady Georgiana Eaton is once again occupying a corner with only one of her brothers to entertain her."

The men chortled.

Kingsley might suffer a broken nose before the evening ended.

The dowager countess sashayed to her grandchildren and dragged Evan to a girl wearing a feathered hairpiece that made her look as though she might take flight at any moment.

As soon as Georgie was alone, a young lad of about ten-and-eight approached her. She held up her wrist, pointed to where her dance card should have hung, and shrugged. William chuckled for the first time since he'd entered the ballroom.

"Looks like the chit is not even in possession of her dance card," Kingsley said.

"I would not bother." Thomas waved a dismissive

hand. "The eccentric thing may be lovely, but she has no interest in men."

Had the arse just referred to Georgie as a thing?

"Speaking of which—" Thomas pinned William in his gaze. "I suspect even the magnificent dashing duke could not bed that girl."

William clenched his jaw until it ached. "Here are your winnings." He rooted in a pocket, then placed a coin purse in Thomas's palm. "You won. I did not bed the lady within the week. However, I will now ask her to dance."

"But she has no dance card." Thomas snorted. "Care to wager? I say—"

"Bugger off," William said.

As he snaked through the crowd, he caught Georgie's gaze and held it as he strolled to her. She smiled and the grumpiness the men had ignited, disintegrated. He bowed and held out his palm.

"My lady, may I have this dance?"

She placed her hand in his and he escorted her to the dance floor.

"You are the most beautiful woman present," he said.

"And you are the most charming man in the world."

As athletic as she was, it should not have surprised him that she was a graceful dancer. She must go out of her way the moments she lumbered about like a brutish man.

"Have my brothers decided to separate you from your balls?" she asked.

Damnation. He loved her unlady-like language.

"They will allow me to remain in one piece.

However, there is a catch."

"Oh?" she asked, worrying those same lips that had done delicious things to his body.

"My darling, how would you like to go on another adventure?"

"Is *My Grace* part of this adventure?" She fluttered her lashes.

Why, the little minx. "Most definitely."

"Where are we going?" she asked.

"We leave for Gretna Green at the stroke of midnight tonight. Just you, Lightning, Burney, and I."

Georgie stood still in the middle of the dance floor. "But that is where couples sneak off to be married."

He nodded. "We do not need to wait for the wedding banns and considering the circumstances, your brothers think it for the best. Despite the prince's discretion, rumors will be rampant by the end of the evening. Alistair packed your bag himself and left it in the stables."

"In that case," Georgie clasped his hand, "let us go."

As much as William wanted to flee the ball with his future duchess on his arm, it was not yet midnight, a room full of people watched like hawks, and two Eaton brothers, both excellent marksmen and possessing strong uppercuts glared from the periphery.

"Not yet." He coaxed her back into their waltz.

She sighed and rested her head against his chest.

He was certain there were gasps from the crowd surrounding them. However, he did not care in the least. He would love his Georgiana no matter how many times she thumbed her nose at propriety.

Once the orchestra crescendoed, she placed her lips

against his ear. "Meet me in the drawing room."

Oh, that raspy voice. She glided to the exit, looked over her shoulder, and smiled. His cock throbbed as he made his way back to the blunderbusses. He would gloat for a moment before taking his leave.

"I dare say, Astleyshire, the girl seems to have taken a fancy to you," Kingsley said.

"Yes, and if any of you cockchafers have anything to say about it, you might want to reconsider." William sent Thomas Merrick a cutting glare. "If you will excuse me, I will take my leave for the evening and head to bed. I had quite an adventurous few days for I recently visited my cousin, *the prince*."

Thomas grinned. "Stories are circulating about you and this Winkentattle chap. Some quite salacious."

William took a heavy step toward the marquess's son, who backed away and held up a palm. "Of course, no one believes the stories."

Not a single man muttered a sound as William walked away.

"If she is naked, you cannot fuck her on the drawing room floor," William whispered as he took the stairs two at a time.

Georgiana stood in front of the fire. A glowing halo surrounded her copper hair and gold dress, making her look like an angel from heaven. She ruined the seraphic image when she grinned mischievously and pointed to the ceiling.

Mistletoe swayed and beckoned. William could not get under it fast enough. She leaped into his arms and their lips locked.

"I love you," he whispered.

"And I, you," she said.

"*Ah, hmm,*" someone murmured from the doorway.

Alistair and Evan stood, arms crossed over their chests.

"Oh, bother." Georgie scowled at them. "Can we just be on our bloody way?"

Alistair sighed. "Harrington, she is all yours now. Good luck."

"Take care of her or I will track you down and disembowel you," Evan said.

Georgie entwined her fingers with William's and planted a kiss on each of her brother's cheeks before dragging him out of the room.

She sprinted down the steps, through the kitchen, and out a back door of Trent Castle. "Hurry," she called as they ran across the yard.

William picked up his pace and overtook her. "Last one there is a rotten plum."

Their laughter echoed through the night as they raced toward the stables.

Epilogue

January 30th, 1817

The blood-red wine was the same color as the rubies encrusting the chalice. The Baron of Deene brought the drink to his lips. At his first sip, something crackled. Then without warning, the legs of his chair gave out, and he crashed to the floor.
From G. E. Tattle's Tales

From its perch on a tree-lined mountain, Hockley Castle overlooked Astleyshire. Even from a distance, the high curtain wall that surrounded the bailey grounds emanated power. Five turrets, as well as a half dozen keeps, and spiraling conicals jutted into the sky.

Georgie pressed her heels into Burney, and they flew across the drawbridge. She halted in front of the Gothic gate and drew in cold air. Her condensation-coated exhale floated upward to a pointed arch where the portcullis met stone.

William and Lightning arrived a few seconds behind her. However, it took a while for the coach containing Millie, Anna, and Lady to catch up.

"'Tis three times the size of Trent Castle," Georgie said to William. "And it looks like something out of a medieval fairytale."

"As long as you stick to the main rooms you will

218

find it as cozy as your home. In fact, we keep the dining room quite warm," he said. "But, once you step outside of the main keep, I cannot make any promises."

Once they were through the gatehouse at least seventy servants in starched forest green livery lined the walkway to the main building. How would she ever manage such a grand house?

A groomsman took Burney's reins, and Georgie leaped to the ground, seeking William's comforting touch. Meanwhile, Millie handed her Lady's leash and Anna smiled at the gathered crowd. A pink-cheeked woman approached and curtseyed. Overwhelmed, it took Georgie a moment to realize that the woman's "Your Grace," was addressed to her.

"Mrs. Benning, I shall give my duchess the tour of Hockley Castle. Would you see to Millie's accommodations? I would like our luncheon to be served in my chambers."

"Of course, Your Grace." Mrs. Benning curtsied again.

By the time Georgie had been introduced to her new staff, her cheeks hurt from smiling. Luckily William was there to steady her because her legs shook as she traversed the great hall with its ornate woodwork and twenty-foot-high ceilings. Long hallways and gray rooms swirled into an intimidating maze. Lady's barks echoed off the stone walls. Georgie's breath caught in her throat. How had she ever thought she could do this?

William's palm squeezed hers, and she forced a smile. His beautiful eyes warmed her soul. She would do this, for him.

"Mayhap you should like to see my favorite places?" he said.

Words escaped her, so she simply nodded and allowed him to carry the puppy as he guided her up a winding staircase. Floral wallpaper in shades of green greeted them on the landing, providing a much-needed respite from the bland stone.

William pushed on a door. "This is my study. I mean, our study."

Georgie gasped. Ceiling-high mahogany bookshelves, holding thousands of books, lined three sides of the room. Triplet Gothic stained-glass windows showcasing every color of the rainbow and a velvet settee that would make a cozy reading nook made up the fourth wall. At the foot of the settee, sat a pink pillow.

William set the pup on the floor. She trotted across the room, turned in two tight circles, and plopped down on her new bed.

William smiled. "I dare say, I think this meets Lady's approval."

Unable to control her glee, Georgie climbed the ladder and plucked a book from the highest shelf that she could reach. "*The Taming of the Shrew,*" she declared with a chuckle.

Deciding she might enjoy reading it for a third time, she clutched the volume beneath her elbow, descended the ladder, and sprang into William's arms.

"This, my darling, is your wedding gift." Grinning from ear to ear, he pointed to one of two mahogany desks. Paper, pens, candles, and an oil lamp had been artfully arranged.

Georgie did a double take and squealed. "Sweetmeats!" She popped one into her mouth and savored the cherry flavor.

After plopping her book beside the silver candy dish, she sat on her throne-like chair and propped her feet on her desk.

William sat at his desk and grinned. "You can pen your stories while I research policy and write proposals to Parliament." He scratched his head and sighed. "I also need to become more involved in the running of my properties and to get out amongst my tenants and workers to get to know them."

Oh, how she loved him. However, she swallowed her treat and stuck out her tongue. "My desk is bigger."

"By five centimeters, if that." He chuckled. "And remind me to have Buttons's head. He was in charge of ordering it and making sure it arrived on time."

"I am of the opinion that he should receive a prize," she said.

Although William rolled his eyes, he could not fool her. Joy oozed from every one of his pores.

"Would you like to see our bedchambers?"

Georgie nodded with so much enthusiasm that a strand of hair tumbled from its confinement.

Much like the combination library study, her bedroom was spectacular. The upholstery, bedding, and curtains were turquoise with tiny yellow roses. Fresh flowers sat on the writing desk and nightstand. And a dressing table festooned with yards of frilly fabric sat beneath another stained-glass window.

"'Tis beyond lovely." She placed Lady in the center of her bed and within seconds the pup was sound asleep.

"But I hope that you will spend your evenings with me." William pushed on a door and invited her into his chamber of rich burgundy and gold.

Four massive posts and a lush canopy of brocade and velvet surrounded the bed where they would make love night after night. A tray of beef sandwiches and pretty cakes had been laid out on a table for them.

Much more at ease, and filled with excitement, Georgie devoured her meal as they talked.

"Are you too tired to see the rest of the castle?" William asked.

"I shall just live in our bedchambers and the study." She stretched her arms to the ceiling and sighed.

"But the best part is still to come."

"Oh?" Georgie's toes tingled as he pinned her in his gaze and removed his cravat.

She licked her lips and waited for him to expose the hard lines of his muscular chest. Instead, he came around behind her and tied the silk fabric around her eyes.

Behind the mask, her senses heightened. His breath flicked across her shoulder like tiny flames and his husky voice landed deep in her belly.

"Let us go."

She tilted her head back and enjoyed the sensuous kisses he placed on her neck. Her heartbeat quickened and her thighs quivered as he helped her to stand. Making love while masked—oh, my!

The bed was only a few feet away so when the door closed behind her, it became apparent that they had left the room.

"William, where are we going?"

"Trust me, darling."

With her life. For he was as loyal as Alistair, as charming as Evan, and as brave as Stephen.

Chilly air blew across her, eliciting a shiver. Their

footsteps which had been muffled now hit stone instead of carpeting. Were they to make love in the dungeons? Well, she had once said she wanted to lie with him in every room of Rosa House.

She bit her lip. Yes. The same was true of Hockley Castle.

After a long trek, William asked, "Are you ready?"

"Yes." He could ravish her wherever they were.

He untied the blindfold and it fluttered to the ground.

She blinked.

They stood in the middle of a *piste*, and the *piste* was in the center of a vaulted, impenetrable room.

"My brother and I turned the casemate into a training ground about two years ago," William said.

No wonder her husband could outwit her in the sport in which she excelled.

Foils, swords, gloves, masks, training pads, and an assortment of training gear had been organized and mounted on the far wall.

"Are you too tired for a quick bout?" he asked.

She bounced onto her toes. "No."

"Splendid. For a duel with my duchess shall whet my appetite for some delicious post-bout activities." He winked.

Georgie grasped the bottom of her skirt and prepared to rip.

"No," William said. "I do love that dress." His gaze slid over the low neckline and her overflowing bosom. He pointed to a curtain. "Behind there you shall find whatever you might need."

Georgie kicked off her slippers and chose a pair of knickers and a cotton shirt.

William lifted the curtain and with heavy-lidded eyes, he watched her change.

"If you do not stop looking at me like that, I should make love to you right here in this dressing closet," she said.

Pulling her to him, he grasped each of her buttocks in his large palms. He squeezed and she squealed with delight.

Lovemaking or fencing? Oh, her life was grand.

"First to achieve five taps wins," he said.

A game that involved both hearts and swords might prove the perfect afternoon.

She pulled on shoes and skipped to the center of the room. Bending her forward knee, she took the ready position.

Mostly their swords clashed. Although occasionally their lips knocked together. William had much difficulty keeping his hands off her breasts and once she grasped and kneaded *My Grace.*

Eventually, William tapped her for the fifth time.

She stomped her foot. "You may have won again, my husband. But I shall make it my life's work to bring you to your knees."

He dropped to the floor in front of her and ran a hand up her thigh. "You already have me at your knees."

Georgie chuckled as she retrieved his discarded cravat. Swinging it between her fingers, she carried it to where he knelt. "I have been thinking…"

"Yes, my duchess?" he asked, his blue eyes glittering mischievously.

She formed the necktie into a blindfold and secured it around her head. William Harrington, the Duke of

Astleyshire hissed and tugged her knickers to the ground.

Thereupon, they enjoyed their late afternoon delight.

A word about the author...

Nicki Pascarella lives in Pennsylvania with her husband, daughter, and hyperactive Shetland Sheepdogs. When she isn't writing fiction, you will find her reading, belly dancing, or running 5ks with her furry partner.

****

https://www.nickipascarella.com/

****

If you enjoyed this story, leaving a review at your favorite book retailer or reader website would be much appreciated. Thank you!

Thank you for purchasing
this publication of The Wild Rose Press, Inc.

For questions or more information
contact us at
info@thewildrosepress.com.

The Wild Rose Press, Inc.
www.thewildrosepress.com